I0621276

Halloween Hustle

A Cassandra Sato Mystery Novella

Kelly Brakenhoff

Emerald Prairie Press

Ebook ISBN 9781957938066

Print ISBN 9781957938073

Also By Kelly Brakenhoff

*H*ALLOWEEN *HUSTLE IS A standalone novella within the Cassandra Sato Mystery series set in rural Carson, Nebraska, at Morton College. There aren't any spoilers and it's okay to read it out of order. If this is your first time reading a story in this series, you might find it helpful to know a bit about some of the recurring characters with speaking parts listed here. Of course there are more characters, but this will give you a head start of knowing a bit about the main characters' backgrounds. Happy reading!*

Morton College Faculty and Staff

- DR. CASSANDRA SATO: Vice President of Student Affairs

- MEG O'BRIEN: ASL Interpreter Coordinator and Cassandra's best friend

- MARCUS FISCHER: Vice President of Facilities and Maintenance, Cassandra's boyfriend.

- ANDY SUMMERS: Morton College Campus Security Director

Students

- RACHEL NAGLE, LOGAN DUNN, BRIDGET: Student workers in Cassandra's office

Carson, Nebraska townspeople

- SHERIFF HART AND DEPUTY SCOTT TATE

- MR. & MRS. GILL: Cassandra's next door neighbors

- SEAN GILL: USDA worker, son of neighbors Mr. & Mrs. Gill

- MARGIE GALLAGHER: owner of The Home Team Bar

- DEREK SWANSON: Reporter from the *Omaha Daily News*

Chapter One

C ASSANDRA SATO, VICE PRESIDENT for student affairs at Morton College, sighed as she stared at the slick health insurance policy brochure. A wellness goal? She pinched the inch of flab on her waist. This new initiative was the last thing she needed. Her daily schedule was packed enough without having to set and track "wellness goals."

She used to be so fit, spending her weekends hiking the tropical trails near Oahu State's campus or catching waves surfing at the beach near her former home in Hawai'i. Now, she barely had time for a 15-minute yoga stretch in the mornings before rushing off to work, and her old wetsuit just took up space in her one-car garage.

The meeting ended, and Cassandra headed over to the Student Center's dining hall. The morning sunlight streamed through the high windows, casting an indirect glow on the array of fruits and muffins set out for the staff's Wellness Fair. She picked up a plate, filled it with food, and turned her attention to the insurance and lifestyle booths lining one side of the room.

"Are you going to eat that muffin?" Andy Summers, the campus security director, asked as he sidled up to the small pub table where Cassandra was eating breakfast after the meeting.

"Trying to," she replied, popping a piece of fruit into her mouth. "But this whole wheat bran muffin thing just isn't as satisfying as a good old-fashioned donut." The chewy, heavy muffin was only tolerable because she was washing it down with her favorite Kona coffee from her travel mug. She glanced over at the insurance booths, feeling a mixture of annoyance and resignation.

"The boss is just trying to help us shed a few pounds," he teased, patting his stomach. "I know I could stand to lose some of this donut weight."

"Me too," she admitted, poking at the fruit on her plate, "but they really are taking this physical fitness thing to extremes. I used to eat so much healthier, but the pressure of this job makes it challenging."

"Ah, yes, the never-ending battle between work and kolaches," His eyes twinkled. "You know, we could try something new together. A little friendly competition."

"Like what?" she asked, one eyebrow raised.

"Let's think it over while we enjoy this delicious, nutritious breakfast." Andy's voice was full of sarcasm. "We'll come up with something."

Might as well face the coming changes head-on, just as she did with everything else in her life. "Let's make a plan," Cassandra said, taking another bite. "Something that suits our schedules and gets us in shape."

They threw away their plates – hers with half a muffin remaining – and slowly walked past the booths.

"CrossFit?" Andy suggested, but she shook her head.

"That's a hard no," she shivered, imagining herself doing pull-ups until she passed out from exhaustion.

"Kickboxing class? Water polo?"

"Those are good, but I want something less ... intense." Cassandra hesitated for a moment, remembering last week when she challenged Meg O'Brien's son Tony to a race around the block. The 10-year-old boy had taken off like a panther, leaving her in the dust. Halfway around the block, she'd been forced to stop jogging and walk because of the stabbing pain under her ribs. At 34 years old, she was embarrassed to admit she couldn't even run around one block.

"Well look at this one!" Andy exclaimed, as they neared a brightly colored booth decorated with skulls and jack-o'-lanterns. "A charity Halloween Hustle 5K run. It's perfect! We can train for it and get fit while helping a good cause."

Cassandra's eyes lit up. "That's ... not horrible. And it'll give me a chance to redeem myself after that humiliating defeat against Tony."

"Ha, I remember you telling me about that. Kid's fast, huh?"

"Like lightning," she replied, rolling her eyes. "But I'm not letting him win again. I used to be athletic, you know."

"Really?" Andy smirked. "I would've never guessed, what with your taste for donuts and kolaches."

"Hey, you're one to talk, Mr. Runza belly," she retorted, poking his midsection teasingly. Andy had been the number one influencer in making her a fan of the local restaurant chain whose specialty was baked meat pies, and it showed. His abs were shaped more like a case of beer than a six-pack, but he took it in stride.

A large sign behind the booth advertised Lee Energy, the corporate sponsor of the fun run. Cassandra took a registration flyer as her gaze zeroed in on Jameson Lee's face plastered across the cover. With hair perfectly coiffed into a gel-swept wave and his toothy grin stretched wide, Cassandra recognized the town councilman from previous community and college events. While she had to admit he was easy on the eyes, beneath that image lurked an arrogant man who always wanted to be the center of attention.

"Don't get me started on that ridiculous magician's hat routine he pulled at the budget meeting," Andy said. "Pulling fake money out of thin air was the dumbest stunt."

"I wish I could forget," Cassandra groaned. "But his dumbest idea was when he wanted to cut funding for library books and replace them with virtual reality headsets!"

It was then that they noticed the perky student with blonde hair wearing a Lee Energy polo shirt and a hundred-watt smile holding a clipboard. "Hi, I'm Patty! Part of my internship duties are planning this charity event for the food bank," she said, pointing to a large plastic crate filled with soup cans and macaroni and cheese boxes. "If you donate a can of food, you get a discount on the registration fee."

Patty offered a glossy postcard to Andy. "Your department can join the team challenge. Teams with the highest participation and fastest race times will win prizes from the Gas and Sweets!"

Another young man with a matching polo shirt offered Patty a disposable coffee cup. "Pumpkin Spice Chai! Your favorite, right?"

Annoyance flashed across Patty's features at the interruption, but she quickly recovered. "My hands are full ... can you set it on the table over there, Tom?"

Tom's face deflated slightly, but he turned and did as she asked before returning to his post behind the booth.

Patty turned back to Andy and batted her spider-sized eyelashes at him, ""The race starts and ends near the Johnson Mansion, one of our company's latest developments. You could personally help me earn a bonus from my boss by recruiting the most people for the event. Can I sign you up now?"

She bounced as she awaited their replies, her enthusiasm much greater than Cassandra's. "We're still thinking about it," Cassandra stalled. "I have the form, thanks."

Patty handed her a business card with a three-digit number written on it. "Okay, sure. I understand. But when you sign up, can you write my referral number on your registration, so I get the credit? I'd really appreciate your support."

Cassandra had been ambitious at Patty's age, but something about the combination of eagerness and pushiness made the hairs on Cassandra's neck rise with distaste. Cassandra and Andy side-stepped away from her, and Patty quickly pursued another staff member.

"How about we make a deal?" Cassandra said. "We give this wellness initiative a real shot. Sign up for the charity 5K coming up next month. If we can finish it, we treat each other to a steak dinner at The Home Team."

Andy's eyes lit up, and for a second Cassandra wondered if his enthusiasm was because of the prospect of getting in shape or going out for steak with her. "Alright, alright," he laughed. "So, we've got ourselves a challenge: the Halloween Hustle 5K. Let's make it interesting. Whoever finishes last buys the first beer."

"A *light* beer. None of those local brews with a gazillion calories."

They moved on to the vendor booths and stood scrutinizing the nutrition labels on various energy bars. "Who knew there were so many flavors of protein bars?" Andy joked. "I mean, do we really need 'Peanut Butter Explosion' and 'Chocolate Lava Party?'"

"Didn't you once eat a donut called 'Chocolate Sprinkle Extravaganza?'" Cassandra retorted, smirking at his hypocrisy.

"Hey, I'm not the one who needs to read every single label," Andy defended himself.

"Fine, let's get these," Cassandra said, handing a box of assorted bars and her credit card to the sales rep. "Now, about our training plan. We should download a Couch to 5K app on our phones."

"Great idea," Andy agreed, pulling out his phone to search for the best-rated app. "And what about our furry friends? Buckley could handle a few miles, but do you think Murphy can keep up?"

"Murphy may have short legs, but he's got spirit," Cassandra said, her voice tinged with a hint of worry. She'd adopted the West Highland Terrier six months earlier, and although he was energetic, she wasn't sure how he would fare on serious runs.

"Sounds like he'll be a perfect match for you, then," Andy laughed, his gaze scanning the length of her petite frame.

"Very funny," Cassandra shot back. Although, truth be told, her "running" was more like fast walking. "But you're right; we should include the boys in our training. They could use the exercise, too."

With their healthy snacks in hand, Cassandra and Andy discussed their training regimen, as they walked back to their respective offices, determined to make the most of the weeks leading up to the Halloween Hustle.

"Alright, let's start with three runs a week," Andy suggested, glancing over at Cassandra for approval.

"Sounds good," she agreed, her mind organizing schedules, meal plans, and workout gear. "I'll need to set aside time for mental preparation as well – visualization exercises, positive affirmations, you know."

"Wow, you're really taking this seriously," Andy said.

"Of course, I am," Cassandra replied, holding out her fist. "I don't just want to finish the race. ... I like my steak cooked medium well, by the way."

"Game on." They bumped fists.

Cassandra felt a tingle of excitement. "Let's meet for our first training run later this week. We'll see who's still standing at the finish line."

Not only would she have a chance to prove herself physically, but she'd also be working toward the wellness goal with a friend. And perhaps, just maybe, she could show young Tony that she still had some fight left in her.

Chapter Two

T HE SUN FILTERED THROUGH the lush canopy above as Cassandra jogged down the winding trail, Murphy trotting beside her. Her thighs burned and her chest heaved, but she kept going. If she was going to whip this body into better shape, she needed to push past the pain.

"Ninety more seconds, then we walk," Andy said, glancing at the timer on his watch. Buckley bounded ahead, chasing a squirrel before looping back. She'd give a hundred bucks for a fraction of the mutt's energy.

Cassandra gritted her teeth as her feet pounded the dirt path. "I can do ninety seconds." If she couldn't handle a simple jog, how was she ever going to finish a 5K? How many miles was that, anyway? While she tried converting kilometers to miles in her head, her breaths rasped in her ears, counting down the seconds.

Andy chuckled, the sound rich and warm. "I know you can. You're one of the most determined people I know."

His praise eased some of her frustration, though she'd never admit it. "Flattery won't make the seconds go any faster."

"Wasn't flattery. Just the truth." His gaze held hers for a beat and her cheeks warmed. She looked away, focusing on the terrain. *What was that about?*

Finally, the timer beeped, and she slowed to a walk, gulping in the fresh air. The damp, earthy scent of the woods soothed her nerves. Birds chirped a merry tune, and a light breeze rustled the leaves.

"That ... wasn't ... so ... bad." Andy pulled a cloth from his pocket and wiped his sweaty forehead. "We'll build up our endurance in no time."

"I know, I know. Patience isn't my strong suit." She gave Murphy's leash a gentle tug as he tried to chase a butterfly.

Andy chuckled again. "I've noticed."

Cassandra shot him a mock stink eye with no real heat behind it. Maybe this whole exercise thing wouldn't be so bad after all, even if the jogging part was miserable. At least the company was decent.

Too soon, the app chimed, and they did another leg of ninety seconds of running. The next time she heard the beep and Cassandra slowed to a walk, Murphy panted beside her, his pink tongue lolling. She swore he was smiling.

"Nice," Andy said, his chest heaving. "We're getting faster."

"If by 'faster' you mean 'still slow,' then yes." Cassandra put her hands on her hips. How could running be so much harder on her lungs than surfing or hiking? "At this rate, I'll be ready to actually run a 5K in about a decade."

Andy slowed and hunched over slightly. "The app promises it'll get easier."

"Well, the app must have the lungs of an Olympian."

They rounded a bend in the trail, and Cassandra stumbled to a stop so abruptly that Murphy continued on, yelping when his leash choked him. Nearby in the ditch, a woman lay on her back., arms flung out to the sides and long, blonde hair fanned around her head. Cassandra gasped quietly, expelling the remaining air in her lungs.

They jogged over and knelt beside her. Andy pressed two fingers to the woman's neck, feeling for a pulse, but he shook his head. "Her skin is still warm," Andy said. "Call 911."

Cassandra fumbled for her phone and dialed, relaying their location to the dispatcher. She kept her eyes on the surrounding area, looking for any helpful details. The woman was dressed in athletic gear like them, as if out for a jog. There were no obvious signs of injury, but a small amount of blood pooled in the dirt under her head.

Cassandra swallowed hard against the sour taste in her mouth. "Not again," she groaned.

"Do you recognize her?" Andy asked. "She looks familiar to me."

Cassandra's gaze flickered over the woman's face. Her eyes widened as she placed the blonde hair and angular features. "Her name's Patty. Remember, from the Wellness Fair last week?"

"Not again," Andy echoed. He ran a hand through his hair, looking distressed. "What is going on in this town?"

Cassandra shook her head, at a loss. In the short time she had lived in Carson, Nebraska, there had been two murders, countless thefts, and general mayhem surrounding Morton College. Maybe she should've taken a job in a nice quiet city where nothing bad happened, like Chicago.

Cassandra sighed, glancing over at Andy. His jaw was set in a grim line as he stared down at Patty's body. Through the trees, she could see the sun rising over the dilapidated property everyone in town referred to as the Johnson Mansion. "Patty was out early this morning, but I wouldn't run back here alone in the dark."

Andy studied her for a long moment, concern etched into his features. "I know that look, but let the sheriff handle the investigation. It's not our job."

Cassandra walked over to Buckley and Murphy, who were sniffing at the bushes a safe distance from the body. She tethered their leashes to a nearby tree before they got any bright ideas about disturbing the scene. The sound of sirens interrupted her thoughts. *About time.*

Within minutes, Deputy Scott Tate jogged up the trail from the direction of the trailhead parking lot. His large, athletic frame moved smoothly, and when he stopped near them, he wasn't even breathing hard.

"Well, if it isn't Carson's busiest amateur detectives," he said, looking unsurprised to see them at another crime scene. He nodded at Patty's body. "I assume this is our victim?"

"Patty, but we don't know her last name," Cassandra said. "I know she's a college student because she mentioned an internship at Lee Energy. We're out on our morning run and just found her."

Tate knew them well enough to know that neither she nor Andy would be running any marathons soon, but his only reaction was to raise one eyebrow skeptically.

Deputy Tate walked over to get a closer look, snapping on a pair of gloves. After several moments, he straightened, gaze sharp. "There's not a lot of blood, but I'd say she's been here at least an hour, minimum."

Cassandra shivered, her own discomfort forgotten in light of this young woman's fate. Unlikely that she'd had a medical emergency. More likely something sinister had happened to the vivacious student.

The volunteer fire department's EMTs arrived at the scene carrying a large duffel bag and a folding stretcher.

Tate asked them a few more questions and took notes on his phone, but soon there was nothing more to add. "We'll handle things from here," Tate said. "But if you remember anything that could help with the investigation, give me a call."

They nodded. As the emergency responders moved in, Andy went back to get the dogs. Handing Murphy's leash to Cassandra, he said. "Come on. Let's get out of their way."

Cassandra let Murphy steer her down the trail, stunned and shaken by their grim discovery. As they walked in silence back to their cars, she tried memorizing every detail she could about the scene, mind churning.

"Please tell me this isn't connected to the college somehow," she said.

"Wish I could, but my mama used to smack my head for lying." Andy ran a hand through his hair. "But we have to be careful. If this turns out to be a murder, the killer won't want us sticking our noses in."

"We can't just ignore it!" Cassandra threw up her hands. "I'm guessing Patty was one of our students. We're responsible for finding out what happened."

Andy sighed, gazing at her with a mixture of fondness and exasperation. "I should have known you wouldn't let this go."

"Never." Cassandra nodded somberly. "So, what's our plan? We should start by talking to people at the college who knew Patty best. Maybe her classmates or the people in charge of her internship. And we need access to her emails, social media, anything that might provide a clue."

"Interviewing suspects is dangerous," Andy warned. "We should leave that to the police."

"We're not interrogating anyone," Cassandra argued. "Just casually chatting to get a sense of their opinions about Patty and who might have wanted to hurt her. We'll keep the police updated if we find anything new."

Andy studied her for a long moment, then sighed again, shaking his head. "You are stubborn."

"It's one of my superpowers."

He turned away, but not before she caught the smirk on his face. She liked messing with him and getting him to laugh. His job required too much seriousness that sometimes seeped into the way he viewed life.

"Alright, I'm with you on this." He held up an index finger for emphasis. "But we have to be extremely careful. Agreed?"

Cassandra nodded. "Agreed. Cautious, but determined to solve the case. Quickly, before the situation gets worse."

Andy groaned. "Famous last words."

Just as they reached the edge of the woods, they spotted a familiar figure leaning against a tree, scribbling in a small notebook. It was Sean Gill, Cassandra's neighbors' son, who worked for Homeland Security in Washington DC.

"Sean!" Cassandra called out in surprise. "What brings you back to town?"

"Hey, Cassandra," he replied, looking up from his notebook with a warm smile. "Just visiting my parents for a few days. What's going on here? I heard there was some kind of commotion."

"You could say that," Andy chimed in grimly. "We found a student on the trail. I'm afraid she didn't make it."

Sean stiffened up and tucked his notebook in his back pocket. "A college student? That's unexpected ... and sad."

Cassandra felt a wave of emotion constrict her throat as they spoke about the tragedy with almost casual indifference. Exchanging glances with Andy, she nodded wordlessly.

Murphy tugged his leash until he was close enough to sniff Sean's pant leg. Sean leaned over and scratched a spot behind Murphy's ear.

Murphy nuzzled his hand and looked like he wanted to go home with Sean. How did dogs remember people so well just by smell?

"Murphy goes on hikes?" Sean raised an eyebrow, intrigued.

"Training run," Andy clarified. "We're doing a 5K run next month." His chest puffed out like he was sucking in his gut.

Cassandra wasn't ready to brag about her jogging prowess to anyone. She barely could run a mile, let alone more. Sean was obviously super fit and probably ran 6-minute per mile marathons in his free time. Uphill. It was time to get home and shower before Sean and Andy's competitive bro thing kicked into another level of bravado. She tugged Murphy away. "Tell your mom and dad hello from me." "Well, if there's anything I can do to help, just let me know." "Will do," Cassandra replied as she got into her car.

On the way home, Cassandra marveled at how quickly the pleasant morning had spiraled into gloom. And the timing of Sean Gill's appearance in town made chicken skin rise into bumps on the back of her neck.

Chapter Three

CASSANDRA SATO SAT IN her office later that morning, absently scrolling through student workers' timesheets as she tried to focus on the tasks at hand. Andy had texted an image of Patty's college ID. A simple enrollment search confirmed Patty Maynard was a Morton College junior majoring in business management with a 3.6 GPA. Andy wrote, "They'll do an autopsy to be sure, but Deputy Tate said the deceased had a head wound and scrapes on her hands."

The media would make the connection to the college immediately. Morton enrollment was already down the past few years. No parent would send their beloved child to campus if they were worried the town is unsafe. But the more she thought about it, the more uneasy she felt.

If Deputy Tate was right about the time of death, Patty was out alone before dawn on an isolated, wooded trail. That sounded unlike the actions of a smart, conscientious student. Something was terribly wrong, and it wasn't just the fact that she had discovered the young woman's body.

Cassandra's thumbs trembled slightly as she texted a reply to Andy. "What if Patty wasn't alone on the trail? That means someone knew she was hurt or already dead and left her body to be found by a passerby."

As much as Cassandra wanted to believe it was an accident, she'd already been through this situation enough times to recognize foul play when the facts pointed in that direction. It seemed absurd to hope the killer was an outsider who had somehow found their way into their tight-knit community. The alternative was worse. Could the murderer be someone she knew? Someone from the college itself?

"Need more coffee to focus." She said out loud, pushing her travel cup under the Keurig spout, and tapping the button. She needed to look at this objectively and not let her emotions cloud her judgment.

Murphy roused from his nap on the corner bed she kept in the office and stared at her expectantly. The whiskers on half his face were smashed where he'd been resting on the cushion.

The phone buzzed on her desk. Her boyfriend Marcus Fischer was out of town for a week bow hunting for deer with his brothers-in-law. She scooped up the phone and opened the call. "Please tell me you didn't hurt Bambi's mother?"

"Not yet. I'm holding out for a big buck, anyway."

Whenever he talked about finding a buck with huge antlers, Cassandra imagined the scene with Charlie Brown sitting in a pumpkin patch waiting for the Great Pumpkin. She smiled.

"I got your text. Are you alright?" Marcus asked. "Finding that woman must have been a shocker."

"I was running with Andy and the dogs, not alone. I'm fine. I just feel so bad for her family and friends. She was too young."

"I'm think I'll come home early."

"Whoa, brah," she spoke quickly. "I doubt the killer was randomly waiting on the trail and happened to meet Patty before dawn."

"If it was another student, I should be there to help."

Cassandra countered, "We'll be fine for a few more days. Finish your trip."

Murphy's brown eyes gazed back at her, and his head tilted a few degrees to the side as though he were listening.

"I can hear your brain churning. You're going to poke around asking questions, aren't you?"

"I'm just curious what could be the motive? Money? Revenge? Or maybe... jealousy?" That the killer could hide in plain sight was unsettling, but she couldn't ignore the possibility.

"Please be careful," Marcus warned. "I don't want you getting hurt."

"Murphy will watch my back," she assured him while dropping a small treat on the floor for Murphy to devour.

Murphy sneezed and scratched an ear before diving into his treat eagerly.

"A twenty pound dog doesn't exactly inspire peace-of-mind," Fischer groaned. "Look I gotta go, but I'll talk to you soon."

"Careful, you'll hurt his feelings," she teased. "He thinks he's ferocious."

After they hung up, Cassandra's eyes narrowed, her fingers tapping rhythmically on her desk. It was time to dig deeper. "I know who to ask first," she murmured, her voice barely audible.

She grabbed the empty watering can alongside her desk and headed to the kitchenette area of the main Student Affairs office suite where several of her work-study students were working and talking. The lively chatter paused upon her arrival, all eyes turning toward her.

"Hey, folks," Cassandra attempted to hide her apprehension behind a warm smile as she watered the college-issued ficus and palm trees. "I have a quick question for you."

"We heard about Patty, Dr. Sato," replied Rachel, an energetic sophomore who had always been eager to please her. "Did you really find her body? Tell us what happened. I'm so scared!"

Cassandra paused and really looked at the undergraduates. More than ten years younger than herself and with long lives ahead of them, presumably. The harsh truth was that until they found out what happened to Patty, there likely was a killer on the loose. Behind Rachel's back, Bridget, an older, slightly more mature senior rolled her eyes at Rachel's enthusiasm.

These students had been exposed to so many mishaps during Cassandra's time heading the office, they just assumed she'd be involved in the investigation of Patty's death.

"We aren't going on a stakeout or anything, Rachel" Cassandra said. "I only met Patty one time, so I didn't really know her. Did any of you notice anything out of the ordinary in the days leading up to ... her passing?" Cassandra stumbled over the last word, acutely aware that she was treading on delicate ground.

For all she knew, they could've been close buddies with Patty, or this situation could bring up unpleasant memories from their childhoods. Besides, pumping her students for background information on a potential murder victim was probably not in the higher education best practices guidebook, wherever that existed.

"Patty would sell her soul if it meant she'd get an A in a class," said Bridget, who was frequently the most skeptical person in the office. "We had to work together on a communication class group project, and she ghosted us for weeks, always with a lame excuse about having to work late. Then when it came time for the final presentation, she took the credit as if the whole thing was her genius idea."

"So, she was overcommitted and ambitious," clarified Cassandra. "Was she acting differently around certain people?"

Bridget went on, "Oh yeah, around faculty or whoever had clout, she was like a saint. But with us, nothing changed since freshman year. We were still her little minions."

Rachel's voice dropped an octave. "You really found her behind the Johnson Mansion? I'll never go near there again."

Logan shivered dramatically. "As haunted as Hogwarts Castle."

"They say Old Man Johnson killed naughty kids and buried them in the woods behind his house near the stream," Bridget said in a spooky voice, waggling her fingers near her face for effect.

Cassandra's eyes widened at the gruesome tale, but a knowing smile crossed Logan's face. "Every kid who grew up in Carson knows that story." He chuckled softly. "Whenever a dog went missing, we used to blame it on Old Man Johnson. Our parents tried scaring us away from playing around the old house," he explained. "But when we were in high school, everyone wanted to hang around and explore for ghosts. Good times ..."

Cassandra narrowed her eyes skeptically. Sometimes they teased her just to see her reaction.

Logan laughed. "Come on, who knows if he did any of those things? Probably just killed some stray cats here and there."

"Alrighty then," Cassandra stalled. "Back to Patty. Did she seem more stressed or distracted lately?"

The students exchanged glances, furrowing their brows as they searched their memories.

"Actually ..." said Logan more seriously, "I saw something odd. Just last week, Patty seemed really nervous during lunch at the coffee shop.

She kept looking over her shoulder and checking her phone, like she was waiting for someone."

Bridget added, "You know Sela Roberts? She stole Patty's boyfriend a while back. But I heard Patty and he were talking again. Wouldn't surprise me if Patty was worried Sela was coming for her man."

"Have you *seen* Sela?" Both of Logan's eyebrows raised. "I mean Patty's pretty and all, but Sela is ..." He gestured with both hands in his chest area as his voice trailed off.

Logan must've noticed the incredulous expressions on the faces of all three women in the office because his cheeks reddened, and he quickly picked up his cell phone and tapped the screen. "Sorry, I remembered I gotta call someone." Jumping out of his chair, he crossed to the doorway in three strides.

"Just, wow." Cassandra shook her head. Sometimes the ten years' difference in their ages felt like thirty. "But really, was Patty seeing anyone that you know of?"

Rachel hesitated, then spoke up. "I overheard Patty arguing with someone on the phone a couple of days ago. She sounded upset, but I couldn't hear who she was talking to or what they were arguing about." She gestured to where two hearing aids were tucked behind her ears, thus explaining how she might miss the actual conversation but still catch the gist of their exchange.

"Thank you for sharing that, Rachel," acknowledged Cassandra. "It might be important. If you remember any other details, let me know."

A short time later, Cassandra stood outside the admin building while Murphy did his business, the fall humidity reminding her of home minus the cooling island breezes. She was joined by Andy, with Buckley in tow. The mutt's wagging tail and eager eyes brought a faint smile to Cassandra's face as she gathered her thoughts.

"Alright," she pulled her focus back to the task at hand. "I've just spoken with some of the student workers, and they had a few interesting things to say about Patty."

"Like what?" Andy frowned slightly.

"Everyone seemed to dislike her. Apparently, she was known to be competitive and ruthless with her classmates," Cassandra shared. "She even had a heated argument on the phone recently, although no one caught the details."

"Sounds like she made plenty of enemies," Andy mused, rubbing Buckley's ears absentmindedly.

"From everything we know about Councilman Lee, it sounds like Patty's personality was a perfect fit for his internship." Cassandra said. "But how much of that came from her and how much did he teach? I can hardly imagine she upset a business associate so badly they'd kill her. She's just a student."

"Deputy Tate said they're working on possible leads," Andy proposed, "but what if this was a crime of passion or opportunity? The murderer could have followed her to the trail."

"Passion makes more sense. If murder was logical," agreed Cassandra, her eyes narrowing thoughtfully. "But we're still missing some pieces of the puzzle. I'd like to chat with Sela Roberts."

Andy raised an eyebrow. "The diplomat's daughter who got kicked out of graduation ceremonies for bringing the airhorn? Intense, drama queen Sela?"

"She got kicked out of graduation because she ignored requests to stop *using* the airhorn. I know no one wants to mess with her mother and the fat donation checks to the college. But apparently, there was a guy ..."

"Say no more," Andy shook his head. "I don't need details. Just let me know if your conversation leads to anything useful for this case."

"Deal." Cassandra said, "I think it's time we paid the councilman a visit and asked him some questions about Patty."

"The dogs are finished watering the grass, right? I'm ready." Andy gestured toward his car parked nearby.

As they walked toward the vehicle, Cassandra said, "It's almost coffee break time. Maybe we can stop at the gas station on the way to his office."

The dogs hopped into the back seat and perched like bronze statues, brightly gazing out their windows at passing students. Andy started the car and adjusted the rearview mirror, "No kolaches today though. We're in training, remember?"

"Training," repeated Cassandra. "I never had a donut slash kolache problem until I met you, brah."

Chapter Four

C ASSANDRA AND ANDY LEFT Murphy and Buckley in the capable care of the Campus Security front office staff and continued to Main Street. They walked side by side, their strides matching each other as they headed toward Lee Energy's office. According to town gossip, Lee Energy had begun as an oil and gas company owned by Lee's father. When Jameson took over, he moved to more sustainable energy businesses like solar and wind power and developed a reputation for cutting corners and disregarding environmental regulations.

Andy was like a younger version of her brother, Keoni. She enjoyed Andy's easygoing nature and their banter – like siblings who knew each other well enough to tease without causing offense.

"At the town council meetings, Jameson Lee always harps on careful spending decisions for the town. I bet his office is decorated with antique store castoffs." Andy joked, a playful glint in his eyes.

"Yeah, only instead of Mid-Century Modern, it's designed in Mid-Century Thrift," she replied with a grin, her expression turning serious as they approached the entrance to Jameson's office.

The building was a one-story, nondescript beige, brick structure on Main Street not far from the gas station. From the outside, it looked completely utilitarian and functional, but when Cassandra and Andy stepped inside, they noticed someone had put in a lot of effort to make it look inviting.

The white walls were tastefully adorned with framed prints of various works of art, while the wood floors were polished to a shine. The waiting room was filled with comfortable chairs upholstered in soft gray fabric and tasteful orange and black Fall accessories. Everything about the place spoke of quality craftsmanship, from its modern lighting fixtures to its sleek reception desk.

"Mr. Lee is expecting you both. I'm Tom, his executive assistant. Please, come this way." She remembered seeing him working at corporate booth with Patty during the Wellness Fair. Tom led them down a short hallway lined with framed photographs of scenic buildings and views around town.

As they walked, Cassandra noted the difference in extravagance between the low-budget town council policies and his own corporate offices. Clearly, Lee didn't practice what he preached to the town council about fiscal frugality.

Lee's fresh-faced assistant wore preppy khakis with a buttoned golf shirt and brown leather loafers. He paused at a small beverage fridge outside the executive office and removed a glass bottle of fancy water. His hand trembled slightly when he handed her the chilled drink. Andy waved him off.

"Swanky," Andy whispered, gazing at an attractive display case full of local souvenirs, including a stunning bronze statue of a bucking bronco and its cowboy rider. Cassandra knew Mr. Lee was a donor to Morton College, but the quiet wealth on display here made her wonder how much further his reach stretched. Maybe she'd speak to the development office about asking him for a larger donation next year.

Tom must have overheard Andy's interest in the display. "The credit goes to Patty," he gushed. "She spent the summer redecorating the corporate offices down to the last detail. Her taste is exquisite." Pride shone in his eyes until he seemed to realize his use of the present verb tense. "Was," he corrected himself quietly and looked down for a few moments to gather his emotions.

"I'm sorry for your loss," Cassandra said gently.

"Thanks. We worked closely together," Tom exhaled and continued down the hall.

"Here we are," Tom announced, opening the door to Jameson Lee's office and stepping aside. Nervously adjusting his thick, dark-framed glasses, he said, "Please, make yourselves comfortable."

Cassandra stepped into the room where a large mahogany desk covered in neatly stacked papers and architectural blueprints dominated the space. As they settled into the plush chairs facing the desk, Andy leaned over and breathed, "Not quite what I imagined."

"Same," Cassandra agreed, her eyes scanning the room. Seeing Jameson's private chambers gave her more questions about his working-class public persona, but they were here for another reason today. "Remember, we're laser focused on clues about him mentoring Patty."

"Okay Sherlock," Andy nodded, just as Jameson Lee glided into the room, the thick carpet muffling the sounds from his shoes.

Mid-forties and dressed in a plaid button down and belted jeans, he looked like he'd just rolled in from a factory shift. "I'm a busy man, so make it quick."

"Thanks for seeing us, Mr. Lee," Cassandra said politely, trying to avoid his hard stare.

"Andrew there made it sound like I didn't have a choice," Jameson muttered, settling into his ergonomic chair. Cassandra had never heard anyone refer to Andy Summers as Andrew, so it took a hot minute for his comment to register. "Heard about my intern, Patty. Real shame what happened to her. Bad timing, too."

A young woman was dead, and his first thought was the timing. Cassandra blurted, "Would there be a better time?"

"Don't twist my words." Deep creases formed between his dark eyebrows. "I just meant there's a lot of things going on now. The Halloween run, reorganizing our office, commercial projects, like that."

"We'd like to know more about the Johnson Mansion project. Was Patty working on that one too?" Andy asked.

"Ah yes," Jameson leaned back in his chair, connecting his fingers together in front of him. "Patty was a real hard worker and a bright girl. I took her on as an apprentice to teach her the ins and outs of commercial development – using the Johnson Mansion as an example. That eyesore has sat vacant for years. Anything Patty suggested was an improvement."

Cassandra worked to keep her facial expression neutral. She knew from town gossip that Jameson's ambitions often led him to bulldoze over anyone who got in his way. However, she had to tread carefully around him because the town often partnered with the college for events and she couldn't afford to alienate a donor. Her elderly neighbors, Mr. & Mrs. Gill once told her that the only reason Jameson Lee was on the town council was because no one else had volunteered this election cycle.

"Can you tell us more about the different plans you had for the mansion?" Andy asked, keeping the conversation focused.

"Unsure what it's to you," Jameson replied, reaching for a stack of blueprints on his desk. "We considered several options, from turning the mansion into office spaces to building a strip mall. I don't know how I'll replace Patty. She was a quick learner, and I don't have time to chase these subcontractors around and check they're doing it right. I've met lots of college students on campus, and none of them are as sharp as her."

"Was there other interest in the property?" Cassandra interjected, unable to keep her curiosity at bay.

"Over the years there's been interest off and on. Old Man Johnson kicked the bucket fifteen years ago. My assistant Tom is actually some sort of relative. Second cousin twice removed type of nonsense," Jameson said. "Johnson's family kept the house tied up in probate for a few years waiting for everyone to agree to sell the place. Dang lawyers got everything they asked for. I don't know why folks even bother with those shysters. They'll be relieved when I scoop it up off 'em."

"So among the options, did you consider historic preservation or the impact on the community?" Cassandra asked with a firmness that lit Jameson's fuse.

"Historic preservation of that shack! Do you know how much it costs to retrofit hundred-year-old plumbing and electrical? Bottom line is what brings in the most money," Jameson scowled. "Of course I'll make sure the town gets the taxes no matter what happens. That should shut down all those naysayers like Margie Gallagher. Patty and me were working together to review all the options."

"Margie Gallagher opposes your purchase of the mansion?"

"That woman's nothing but trouble. Thinks she knows better than everyone else," Jameson scoffed. "Now without Patty's input, I'm inclined to demolish the dump and start from scratch."

"You'd tear down the whole thing. Won't that have to be approved by the town council?"

"If I buy the place, I'm the final decision maker," he smirked. "I can convince the other three members to support me. Besides, they don't have to like me; they just want my money. "

Cassandra exchanged an uneasy glance with Andy. "Thank you for your time, Mr. Lee,"

"Of course," Jameson's face softened into a satisfied smile. "By the way, did you folks join our company's Halloween 5K run? The teams look good this year. Patty was my point person on that event, but now I'll have to finish it myself."

She and Andy stood up to go. "Yes, we've been training," Andy said with more gusto than she felt.

Cassandra forced a smile. She wouldn't brag about her jog-walking to anyone yet.

Jameson chuckled. "I'm sure. I'll be looking for you two on race day. It's always good to have a little competition."

As they left his office, Cassandra felt Jameson was holding back details. If they wanted to get to the bottom of Patty's murder and learn the fate of the historic property, they'd have to look elsewhere.

Cassandra and Andy walked into The Home Team, the atmosphere immediately embracing them with warmth and laughter. The bar was cozy, filled with locals who were clearly regulars, and the aroma of burgers and beer filled the air.

"Talk about a change of scenery," Andy said, grinning as he looked around. "This is definitely more my style than Jameson's office."

"I didn't realize Rustic Beer Lodge was a style," Cassandra smirked, her eyes scanning the room for Margie Gallagher. She spotted her behind the bar, chatting animatedly with a customer while pouring a beer from the tap. "There she is."

The Home Team décor was a time capsule of Carson history. Local sports team pennants, jerseys, vintage newspaper articles, and signed photos papered the walls in nostalgia. The owner, Margie, was like the unofficial town historian.

As they approached, Margie beamed at them with a warm smile. "Cassandra, Andy! What brings you two here?"

"Hey, Margie," Andy said, leaning against the bar. "We're actually here to talk to you about the Johnson Mansion."

"Ah, that old place," Margie sighed, wiping her hands on a towel. "Such a beautiful piece of history."

Cassandra nodded. "It looks like the property was empty for ages, but now people are showing an interest in what will happen to it."

"I've had my eye on it for years, but first I'd have to win the lottery," Margie chuckled. "No telling why Jameson Lee suddenly got in a snit to buy it. My bartender Joe joked the weasel got bored plucking the wings off crickets in his spare time. At first, the councilman was hot to tear it down. But once me and the historical society had a few meetings with him, he went along with our vision, though a bit scaled down. Now he's all swept up in the idea of leaving behind his legacy," Margie used air quotes when she said *legacy*.

"Is it on the historic register?" Cassandra asked.

"Unofficially. Charles Johnson built his mansion in the late 1800s. He was the town banker and a founding father whose wife Mary Jane made it a gathering place for the community back in the day—parties, fundraisers, you name it. That house has seen it all."

Andy whistled. "Wow. I bet the water and electrical is really outdated."

"Copper pipes," Margie agreed. "The last Johnson of any note was a local lawyer in the 1970s who had a slew of kids and spruced it up to modern times. He lived there until he passed on, but his kids had scattered all over by then." She pointed to a black-and-white photo that hung on the wall behind the bar. Squinting, Cassandra could make out the Johnson Mansion decked out for what looked like a wedding reception with people wearing their best clothes posing out front and white bunting in all the windows.

Margie sighed fondly, "It's because of the sense of community that I've been so fired up to keep the old place standing."

Jameson had mentioned nothing about the historic register - officially or not. But he was the one with the bank account large enough to purchase the place.

"If you won the lottery tomorrow, what would you do with the property?" Cassandra asked.

"Now that's easy," she grinned. "My dream is to set up a bed-and-breakfast. I'd always thought I'd like to own one, and Carson could use more tourist attractions. It would also help to keep the place preserved, y'know? What good's history if we don't remember it?"

"Sounds like a lot of work," Andy said.

"Sure does," her eyes lit up with enthusiasm. "And it's not just the B&B. One of Jameson's stipulations was that we need to turn a profit. We've talked to other tenants like a gift shop and event space too. If it comes off, this will be one heck of an addition to our town!"

Cassandra mulled over Margie's words, considering how they fit into the puzzle surrounding Patty's murder and the future of the Johnson Mansion. There was clearly more at stake here than just a simple property dispute or development project. Jameson's comments about Margie and her group's dream weren't nearly as definitive.

"Your plan seems pretty detailed," Cassandra said. "Like more than just a lottery dream."

"Jameson and me have been talking for months. We have a verbal agreement," Margie continued, her voice wavering slightly. "He said he'd lease me the kitchen and main bedrooms of the house. I bought the perfect curtains at an auction last week."

"Have you signed any paperwork?" Andy asked, furrowing his brow.

"Still unofficial," Margie admitted, fiddling with the edge of a coaster. "But we shook hands on it. And bottom line, we're both business owners trying to better our community."

Half an hour later, Cassandra and Andy stood on the sidewalk, watching a young mom walk her large black Lab while pushing a double stroller.

"I got the impression Jameson hasn't gotten around to telling Margie he wants to remove the house and start over." Cassandra said.

"Unfortunately, in the world of business, a handshake isn't always enough," Andy said. "I'm surprised Margie didn't ask for more formal paperwork. As a business owner, she should know better."

"Maybe they weren't to that level of agreement yet." Cassandra felt a pang of sympathy for Margie, who seemed genuinely invested in her dream of transforming the mansion.

Andy's warning echoed in Cassandra's mind, and a sense of dread crept over her. Jameson's deal had more moving parts than she'd originally thought. If it went wrong, the repercussions would be felt hard by those nearby.

Chapter Five

C ASSANDRA AND ANDY STEPPED out of the car, shielding their eyes from the bright sun. The running trail where they found Patty ran near the decrepit Johnson Mansion, its once grand exterior now worn by time and neglect. Surrounded by ten acres of lush greenery, it stood like an ominous Hollywood haunted house stage set.

"Can you believe the trail back there is so accessible, but the rest of this place is completely overgrown?" Cassandra mused, peering into the thick foliage. "This place gives me the creeps."

"Usually someone hosts a Halloween party on the main floor, and when I was little the mansion was on the main trick or treating circuit. There's no signs or decorations this year. Must be because of the pending real estate deal," Andy replied with a shrug. "A little bit of danger can be fun in the right doses."

As they walked along the edge of the property, they discovered a stream, its gentle gurgling masked by the rustle of leaves. A family of deer grazed in the underbrush, unperturbed by their presence.

"Wow, they're so close!" Cassandra whispered, pointing at the deer. "Aren't they afraid of us?"

"They're used to the trail traffic," Andy said. "Let's look on this side of the stream for any clues about Patty's murder. The sheriff's office could have missed something."

"It's already been a week since we found her body, and they haven't announced any arrests."

"Sheriff Hart and Tate are careful. They don't want to mess up their investigation by leaking details too soon."

They cautiously continued their exploration, careful not to startle the wildlife. Moving closer to the mansion, the air grew heavier, shadows concealing years of secrets. They exchanged glances, nodded, and entered the dark, cavernous house through the unlocked back door.

Inside, a musty smell hung in the air, and creaky floorboards protested underfoot. Eerie paintings adorned the walls, draped in layers of dusty cobwebs. Clearly the mansion held countless stories, but which one would lead them to the truth behind Patty's death?

Cassandra tried not to think about the ghost stories the students had told her about Old Man Johnson. The tales about lights turning on at odd hours or bones buried on the property could be easily explained by vandals or people illegally dumping their pets.

"Hello? What are you two doing here?" a sharp voice cut through the silence, making Cassandra's stomach do a giant somersault. A hippie-styled woman in her forties emerged from one of the many rooms, eyes narrowed. Her petite frame made her look deceptively fragile, but her straight posture showed a confident strength she seemed prepared to use.

"The back door was unlocked," Cassandra felt unusually flummoxed. The woman's eyes held a glint of Bellatrix Lestrange-level mischief.

"I'm the Morton College security director, Andy Summers," Andy said in the same tone Cassandra had heard him use on students who pulled the fire alarm in the dorms. "Who are *you*?"

"Loretta Anderson, Carson Real Estate. And this is Amanda Bauer," she said in clipped phrases gesturing toward a second woman who appeared in the doorway behind her. Loretta's dyed platinum hair was pulled back in a tight bun, and her jade green dress fell to mid-calf. The second woman wore faded jeans and a white t-shirt with Converse low tops and clutched a clipboard. She looked more like a cleaning woman than a prospective customer, but Cassandra wasn't nosy enough to ask more.

The realtor sized up the two trespassers with equal parts suspicion and curiosity: "This is private property," Loretta said firmly as she crossed her arms in front of her chest. "You have no business being here."

"No worries, Loretta," Andy said. "We're just looking around, trying to piece together what happened to Patty Maynard."

"Margie Gallagher mentioned a plan to fix up this place and lease it out," Cassandra said. "Are you two part of that project?"

"We're here for a client," Loretta replied, her tone guarded. "But I don't see how that's any of your business. Don't get in our way. This renovation is important for the future of the town." With that, the women disappeared down a corridor, leaving Cassandra and Andy speechless in the front room.

Cassandra glanced at Andy, weighing their options. "Maybe we can get more information from them," she whispered.

"Let's give it a shot," he agreed, and they followed the ladies down the corridor.

"Excuse me, Loretta?" Cassandra called out, stepping into what appeared to be an old study. The younger woman was measuring the space, her brow furrowed in concentration. Loretta turned around, her expression a mix of annoyance and suspicion.

"What do you want now?" she asked.

"Look, we understand you're busy," Andy began, "but any information you have could be crucial to our investigation."

"Really? You think I know something about that poor girl's murder?" Loretta scoffed, rolling her eyes. "She answered phones and did errands for Jameson, dropping off paperwork ... like that. I barely knew her."

"Even the smallest detail could help us," Cassandra insisted, trying to keep her voice level. "What about you?" she asked, addressing Amanda, who hesitated before shaking her head.

"I don't know anything," Amanda mumbled, avoiding eye contact.

Cassandra wanted to ask if she was a customer or an employee, but something about Loretta's attitude made her hold back.

"See?" Loretta said smugly. "Now if you'll let us get back to work ..."

Cassandra spotted a rolled-up blueprint on the floor. "Wait! Is this part of the renovation plan?"

"Give me that!" Loretta snatched it away, her face reddening. "It's none of your business!"

"What are you hiding?" Andy demanded, narrowing his eyes.

"Excuse me?" Loretta snapped. "Our work has nothing to do with your investigation, so just leave us alone!"

Cassandra half expected Loretta to pull a wand out of her tote bag and curse them.

"Fine," Cassandra sighed, exchanging a defeated glance with Andy. As they walked away, though, she felt strongly that something was off.

"Did you notice the way Loretta reacted when she saw that blueprint?" Andy asked, once they were out of earshot.

"Exactly," Cassandra nodded. "It's like she was trying to keep us from seeing it."

"Maybe there's something about the renovation plans that we're missing," Andy suggested, his brows furrowed in thought. "We should take a closer look at the mansion and see if there's anything odd."

"Let's split up," she suggested.

"Sounds good. Meet you in ten."

They went their separate ways, each determined not to miss any critical clues.

Grateful she had changed into sensible flat shoes, Cassandra searched the rooms. What could Loretta be hiding? Was there a connection between the renovations and Patty's murder?

Cassandra stood in the middle of the grand ballroom, her gaze sweeping across the dusty chandeliers and faded wallpaper.

"Any ghosts?" Andy's voice from the doorway startled her enough to make her squeak and jump an inch. As he entered the ballroom, his footsteps echoed on the creaky floorboards.

"No missing dogs or children," she said, remembering the students' stories about the haunted house. "Just a bunch of antique furniture covered in cobwebs. Those back bedrooms have nasty mattresses and beer bottles like people have been using it as a free hotel."

"Me neither," he admitted, perching himself on a dusty windowsill. "But I've been thinking... what if the plan to subdivide the mansion was Patty's idea?"

"Interesting," Cassandra raised an eyebrow.

"Think about it. She was ambitious, like Jameson, and young enough to have friends getting married or needing event spaces. What if she wanted to manage something like this?"

Cassandra crossed her arms, considering his theory. It wasn't too far-fetched, and it would explain why Patty had been so involved with the Johnson Mansion project.

"Okay, let's say you're right," she said finally. "That still doesn't tell us what Jameson's plan is for the mansion now."

"True," Andy agreed, rubbing his chin thoughtfully. "But it might mean there's someone else who knows more about the renovation plans. Maybe even someone who could help us figure out what really happened to Patty."

"Like Loretta?" Cassandra asked, remembering the realtor's evasive behavior earlier.

"Maybe," he said hesitantly. "Or maybe someone else we haven't met yet."

"Either way, I think we need to dig deeper into the renovation plans and find out who else is involved," she decided, her determination renewed. "If there's one set of blueprints, more copies are somewhere."

Andy nodded. "But first, I'll check out Loretta and her customer. They might be our best leads right now. I'll keep you posted."

With every step, the pressure mounted. And as they left the eerie ballroom behind, Cassandra worried that this time, her usual approach might not work. Would her ninja problem-solving skills find the answers they needed or lead them smack into danger?

Chapter Six

A COUPLE DAYS LATER, Cassandra's phone buzzed on her desk, the screen lighting up with an email notification. She glanced over and saw it was from Derek Swanson, that pesky reporter from the *Omaha Daily News* who always seemed to be sniffing around for a story. Grumbling under her breath, she opened the email, her curiosity piqued despite her annoyance.

"Hey Cassandra," the email began. "Thought you might find this interesting. While researching my latest story on new business developments in town, I came across a signed memorandum between Lee Energy and a demolition company for ... drumroll please ... the *Johnson Mansion!!*"

Derek's unnecessary drama notwithstanding, Cassandra scanned the document. "Jameson Lee," she muttered, reading the developer's signature with disdain. She leaned back in her chair, crossing her arms over her chest. "You slippery snake."

Her movement alerted Murphy, who had been napping in his little dog bed. "You're not the snake, Murph'," she reassured him. His baleful brown eyes stared her down until he felt satisfied with his nonverbal scolding and laid his head back down on the bed. Cassandra shrugged because she was still inept at translating his expressions. She'd never be a dog whisperer.

She turned back to Derek's email and continued reading. "Check the bottom of the document where it lists the contact person's name. Isn't she the college intern who died a couple of weeks ago? Do you know anything about this property?"

Not only did the memo confirm Lee's intention to destroy the historic mansion, it also mentioned Patty by name as a contact person. Cassandra wondered why Jameson had entrusted an intern with such an important task.

Cassandra scoffed, shaking her head. "As if I'd tell you anything that might end up in print," she mumbled, debating whether to reply. But curiosity urged her to dig deeper into the situation.

Cassandra recalled her and Andy's conversation with Jameson. His answers had been so vague, skirting around the truth. It dawned on her that he'd been stringing Margie Gallagher along with false promises of partnership while secretly plotting to demolish the old building. He'd blamed his change of heart on Patty's death, but that didn't seem to be the case.

"Who does he think he is?" she said aloud as though Murphy could understand her. "Playing both sides like this ..." Cassandra felt more annoyed than disappointed.

As much as she tried to see the good in people, Cassandra felt judgmental toward Jameson. She recalled the handful of times when she had seen him show kindness to others, but most of the time he was just a slick, arrogant man, and she couldn't shake her dislike for him.

She knew from seeing him around meetings in town that Jameson had lost his wife a decade ago. "Still," she said, "just because he's had a rough go of it doesn't mean he gets a free pass to double-cross Margie."

She tried to muster some compassion, picturing him alone in his big house, but it was difficult. Especially when she pictured Margie's kind face and dreams of turning the mansion into a bed-and-breakfast. Cassandra admired her dedication to running her businesses in ways that benefited everyone, not just her own pocketbook.

As Cassandra weighed the situation, she knew she couldn't let this injustice slide. The other day when she and Andy had looked around the running trail and house, she'd been distracted and edgy. The pushy vibe from Loretta the realtor had only made it worse.

Maybe if Cassandra went back to the mansion alone, she could take her time looking for evidence about who wanted Patty out of the picture and why.

"Alright, Derek, you want some info?" she muttered, typing out a carefully worded response that revealed nothing of value. "Let's see how much you can dig up on your own."

With a satisfied smirk, she hit send and hooked Murphy up to his leash. If Jameson could play games with people's lives, then so could she – but for the right reasons.

"He's got no idea who he's messing with," she told Murphy. She was determined to uncover the truth. No matter where it led her.

She changed into running shorts and shoes and drove to the same trailhead where she'd parked the day she and Andy ran together with the dogs. She hadn't returned to this spot since they'd found Patty. But the sun would set in an hour, and she needed to get in a two-mile training session. She reminded herself that eventually she'd have to get comfortable being on the trail again, and even though Murphy was small, his bark might scare off any wild animals. Or ghosts.

Ten minutes later, she rounded a bend and came face to face with Deputy Tate. "Howzit?" she asked, hands on her hips, lungs gasping for breath, trying but failing to sound nonchalant.

Built like a college linebacker, Scott Tate's athletic frame might make people assume he was all brawn. Cassandra had worked with him enough to know that he was studying to get his master's degree and that someday he'd probably be the sheriff instead of a deputy.

"You really are running, huh?" he said. "I just assumed you were poking around where you don't belong again. I hear you talked to Margie and Loretta?"

"You're the expert. I wouldn't poke around in your investigation," Cassandra said defensively as they stood on the running trail behind the Johnson Mansion. Had he spotted her car in the parking lot and come looking for her? Seriously. "I was asking those folks about something related to the mansion. I mean ... we found Patty on the trail, not inside the house."

"It's not your job to decide what's important to the investigation."

"I trust you, but it's been more than a week. And where--"

Deputy Tate's eyes narrowed.

"Just answer me this: are you working with Sean Gill?" Yes, Sean did visit his parents occasionally, but his presence in town seemed timely.

Was Sean interested in the commercial development of the house or the murder investigation?

"You need to leave this to the professionals."

Cassandra rolled her eyes inwardly, determined not to let him see her frustration. "Fine," she muttered under her breath.

"Look, just be safe, alright?" His tone softened slightly, though still stern. "This is serious business. We haven't made any arrests yet."

"I noticed," Cassandra said. She felt a bit unsettled by his warning and had doubts about continuing her own investigation.

"Good," Deputy Tate nodded, his gaze lingering on her for a moment before he turned to walk away.

She finished the two miles by walking/running in cycles for fifteen minutes total before she switched to walking only. Wiping herself off with a towel from her backseat, she made an impulsive decision to revisit the Johnson Mansion alone. The path through the trees to the house was just a quarter mile away. "I'll call it our cooldown walk," she told Murphy.

As they approached the back of the mansion, the students' ghost stories and the shadows sent tingles up her back. Marcus Fischer was home from his hunting trip and they'd gone out the night before so he could fill her in on the stories of losing arrows and the big buck that got away. She pulled out her phone and sent him an insurance text. "In case I miss your call, I'll be near the Johnson Mansion for a few minutes, and I'll contact you later." If for some reason Cassandra ran into a giant spider or killer clowns, at least Fischer could tell them where to start searching for her body.

"Great, now I'm playing into some bad horror movie cliché," she whispered with a mix of annoyance and amusement. Determined to understand the situation better, she tried the front door handle, her heart pounding with each creak of the porch's wooden boards. Locked, as expected. Undeterred, Cassandra circled the house until she found an open window. "Here goes nothing," she muttered, hoisting first Murphy, then herself up and through the narrow opening. She tapped the flashlight icon on her phone.

Once inside, the eerie atmosphere intensified, yet there was an undeniable charm hidden beneath the years of neglect. She shivered, suppressing a chuckle at the thought of being a character in a cheesy horror film. "We're both gonna need baths when we get home," she told Murphy as he sniffed under furniture and in corners draped with cobwebs.

She was only here to get a better feel for the place she reminded herself. "Why would anyone kill Patty over this?" she whispered as she explored the second-floor bedrooms. Patty's name was on the company memo, and the development plans must have been filed with the town clerk's office where employees or others could read it. Someone who didn't want Lee Energy's plan to succeed could have seen the paperwork.

As she had noted when she and Andy walked through, the house had large rooms and intricately carved woodwork. The high ceilings were a plus, except where a gaping hole in the entryway roof allowed leaking water to stain the flooring. Her flashlight revealed a large bird's nest tucked between exposed rafters.

Margie and Patty must've had special renovation superpowers to visualize this place as beautiful. Cassandra tried and failed to picture a charming bed-and-breakfast with the community bustling around it. However, the thought of Jameson destroying such a historic building left a sour taste in her mouth.

Maybe she just wasn't cut out for the whole "heartless developer" mindset.

Cassandra tiptoed through the dark hallway, imagining a headless ghost lurking around the corner while chicken skin bloomed on her forearms. The peeling wallpaper and warped floorboards did nothing to put her at ease. Through an upstairs window, she caught a glimpse of orange on the grass outside the back of the house.

Her heart knocked against her ribs while she debated whether she'd seen a real person or if the creepy vibe had gotten to her. With the tree cover, the remaining sunlight was filtered to a gloomy dusk.

"This is madness," she cursed herself for sounding like one of those hapless horror movie characters. She skipped down the stairs as quickly as she dared, given the weak floorboards and potential to fall through two stories to the concrete basement. Rounding the corner, she nearly collided with a man in a bright orange vest, clutching a clipboard. She yelped in surprise.

"Ope!" The man who was definitely not a ghost said. "You're a real person."

"So are you." Cassandra took a deep breath to calm her nerves and adjusted her grip on Murphy's leash, worried he might go into bodyguard mode. One glance downward showed she was way off base. Instead of growling or barking, Murphy gazed at the man adoringly, ears perked up as though expecting a treat.

Maybe if she asked casually, this guy would give her some information about the status of the real estate deals. "Are you working with Loretta and Jameson on this project?"

"Uh ... ma'am," he said, scratching his head and eying Murphy. "I'm just here to survey the site, and I saw your light in the windows." He chuckled, "Thought you were a ghost and wanted to see up close."

"I left my coffee mug somewhere a few days ago, and I'm here retracing my steps." She felt guilty for being caught snooping without permission. "I remember seeing the blueprints the other day, but I don't recall what this area is supposed to become. By any chance, do you have an extra copy of the blueprints?" She asked, hoping to distract him into giving away Loretta's secrets.

"Blueprints? We're not at that stage yet." He looked puzzled. "I'm just getting measurements and such."

"Right," Cassandra said skeptically, raising an eyebrow. She just wanted to know if Loretta was working with Jameson, Margie, or someone else, but she couldn't get a straight answer out of anyone. "For Lee Energy?"

The surveyor glanced around as if searching for an answer in the dusty corners of the front sitting room. "Can't say, really. I'm just doing my job. Wanted to make sure the ghosts weren't having an early Halloween party." He chuckled.

"Of course," she muttered, her frustration growing. Instead of pressing him further and risking him suspecting her of doing something wrong like breaking and entering, she shifted the conversation toward more innocuous topics.

"Nice weather we're having this week, huh?" She offered, trying to sound casual.

"It's warm for October! Perfect for surveying," he agreed eagerly, launching into a lengthy monologue about his favorite local TV meteorologist, the upcoming country band concert he couldn't wait to attend, and his undying love for the cherry kolaches from the Gas and Sweets.

While she couldn't fault him for his bakery weakness, as the minutes ticked by, Cassandra found herself nodding along to his stories while internally screaming for any useful information. But it seemed the chatty surveyor simply had nothing of value to offer.

"Welp," he finally said, checking his watch. "I should probably get back to the office. Good luck finding your mug. Nice chatting with you!"

"Likewise," Cassandra replied, forcing a smile as he disappeared out the front door and gathered his equipment. She leaned against the wall, letting out a frustrated sigh.

Well, that was fifteen minutes of her life she'd never get back. Worse, she was still no closer to finding out what was really going on with those blueprints. Or which developer would end up with the mansion.

The surveyor's truck disappeared down the driveway, leaving Cassandra alone with her reservations. She turned back to face the hallway to the kitchen areas. "Alright, you creepy relic," she muttered under her breath, "let's see what secrets you're hiding."

Murphy's toenails echoed softly through the empty hallway, the peeling wallpaper and dusty floorboards a lonely testament to the family that had once filled the rooms. As they rounded a corner, she spotted an open doorway leading to the dimly lit study. The air was heavy with the scent of old leather and damp wood, making it difficult for her to breathe.

"Ugh," Cassandra grimaced, pulling her shirt collar over her nose. "I could use one of those fancy air fresheners right about now."

Murphy pulled on the leash outside the study and growled. "I'll give you a treat when we get back to the car," she promised him.

She cautiously stepped into the study, her eyes scanning the room for anything unusual. Murphy whimpered. Cassandra stifled a scream and held tightly to the leash, pressing herself against the cold wall for support.

"Jameson?" Cassandra whispered, staring down at the lifeless body of Jameson Lee sprawled across the dusty floor. The cause of his death was obvious: the bloody gunshot wound in his side was hard to miss. She hesitated, then cautiously approached him, her stomach churning at the ghoulish idea of touching him.

After long moments of watching his chest and seeing no movement, she closed her eyes and summoned her calm composure under stress. "What are the odds," she muttered, pulling out her phone and dialing Deputy Tate's number. Her fingers trembled as she held the phone to her ear, suddenly feeling very vulnerable in the eerie quiet of the mansion. Murphy did a faint whine that echoed Cassandra's fear.

"Scott, this is Cassandra," she whispered, doing her best to keep her voice steady. "I found Jameson Lee's body at the Johnson Mansion. You need to get here right away."

"Jameson Lee, for real? This isn't a good time to joke." Tate's tone was skeptical.

"Yes, I'm serious. How could you think I'd joke about finding another dead person? I don't know why this stuff happens to me ..."

Bile and reality climbed her esophagus, a moist heat wave rushed into her head, and the salad she ate for lunch jolted back up. Dropping the phone, she hurried to the kitchen and retched into the ancient sink. She rested her damp forehead on her arms until the heaving subsided, then used the bottom of her t-shirt to wipe her mouth.

Scooping up her phone, she cleared her throat. "Are you still there? Sorry, I ..."

"I heard you. Go outside and wait on the front porch," Tate instructed. "And don't touch anything. We're on our way."

Moving automatically, she did as ordered. The chilly breeze instantly sharpened her senses when she reached the front steps and sank to the wooden stoop. As the adrenaline worked its way through her jumpy limbs, she looked at her phone screen. She could let Fischer know about Jameson, but he'd probably just give her a hard time for being in this predicament again. She put away the phone and scratched the soft hairs behind Murphy's ears while they waited.

Unfortunately, since Cassandra had moved to Carson, she'd called 911 often enough to know that it took a while for the volunteer fire department and the county sheriff's people to arrive at an emergency scene.

Dusk settled like a blanket around them, the trembling of leafy branches and mysterious shadows on the weed-filled lawn making Cassandra skittish. Murphy was just as jumpy, undoubtedly taking his cues from her palpable anxiety. She had to get a grip.

Everything had to be connected, somehow: Patty's death, Margie's plans, Loretta's blueprints, and now Jameson. As she waited for Tate to arrive, Cassandra replayed her earlier interaction with the surveyor. Hopefully, the police would dig into how long he'd been at the house and if he was really a surveyor or not? Given the timing of his visit, he could have something to do with Jameson's death.

Her thoughts were interrupted by the sound of sirens approaching in the distance. Before the first cruiser or ambulance pulled up to the mansion, Cassandra steeled herself, ready to make her statement to Deputy Tate. But instead of Tate, the first car to park in the driveway was a plain silver Honda that looked vaguely familiar. The driver's door opened and out stepped none other than Sean Gill.

"Well, of course, Sean would be here right when I find a dead body," she muttered. "Perfect timing, as always."

She wearily watched him approach the porch. "I guess we can stop pretending your visit home is a coincidence?"

"Who's pretending?" Sean asked. "You just called in a homicide, am I right? The second time in as many weeks. I don't have to feign an interest in who's disturbing my peaceful hometown."

"It's a relief knowing you're on the job, because it means their deaths are part of a larger investigation and not random crimes. I hope you'll be doing everything you can to protect our student population."

But while Sean was on the case, would he be working with or against her?

Chapter Seven

C ASSANDRA STOOD ON THE bustling Main Street, watching as the townspeople went about their daily routines. She sighed, her breath visible in the crisp, morning air, a reminder that it would be months until the next warm season. Times like these she missed her tropical home and the consistently warm weather.

"Thanks for meeting me. I needed an active break after not sleeping much last night. It's hard to believe Jameson Lee is actually gone," Cassandra said, rubbing her arms for warmth.

Andy nodded solemnly, his eyes scanning the sidewalks like he always did. Her boyfriend Marcus Fischer and her friend Connor O'Brien did the same thing. It must have something to do with the military or law enforcement experience. They all seemed to have a sixth sense alert to the vibe of the surrounding area. For Cassandra, the result was usually a reassuring feeling that someone had her back.

"I followed up with Sela Roberts to see what kind of dustup she and Patty had gotten into about their ex-boyfriend," Cassandra told Andy the shortened version of the long and dramatic conversation. "Let's just say that Sela has moved on." Actually, Sela had called the guy a major suck-up and said that Patty was welcome to him, but Andy didn't need to know the whole story.

"I've been asking around," Andy replied, "trying to get a feel for how people felt about Jameson. Seems he didn't have many buddies."

"He was a hard person to like," Cassandra agreed. "Although I hope people will remember that he used his money to sponsor good things like the charity 5K run and wasn't always a slimeball."

"Money can't buy everything," Andy said with a shrug. "Anyway, we should head over to The Home Team. I want to know Margie Gallagher's thoughts on all this."

As they entered the warmly lit bar, the sounds of conversation and cutlery on dishes welcomed them along with the scent of bacon and eggs. Margie was behind the counter, bent over a clipboard full of papers. Her eyes lit up over her cheater reading glasses when she saw them, and she waved them over.

"G'morning," Margie greeted them, not quite her usual bubbly self. "What brings you by?"

"Hi, Margie," Cassandra replied, forcing a smile. "Can we talk to you for a few minutes?"

"Sure, what's up?" Margie replied, coming around the bar and indicating an empty table near the wall. They pulled out the wooden chairs and sat. Nearby a group of retired farmers ate breakfast and another table of salt-and-pepper haired women busily wound yarn from skeins into balls while they chatted.

Andy lowered his voice. "We're trying to understand what happened with the Johnson Mansion and Jameson."

Tears filled Margie's eyes, and she dabbed at them quickly with a bar towel she'd pulled from her apron. They gave her a moment until she cleared her throat and nodded at him to continue.

"A few days ago, you mentioned a verbal agreement to keep the property intact and renovate the house."

"Oh, yep. Jameson and his so-called 'verbal agreement.'" Margie made air quotes as angry red splotches appeared on her cheeks. Her gray hair was pulled back into a simple ponytail, and she wore no makeup on her pale skin. "That double crosser promised me that if I helped him with the catering for his events, he'd restore the Johnson Mansion and let me turn it into something amazing."

"What do you mean, double crosser?" Cassandra asked.

"A reporter called me the other day. He's working on a story about Jameson's company and all the deals he had in the works for the area. Turns out Jameson was planning to tear the mansion down and put in a strip mall of all things!" Margie's voice was loud enough to draw the attention of the nearby knitters. There was a brief pause in conversation as she glared back at her patrons. Then more buzzing as the group returned their gazes to the table and no doubt dissected that new piece of information.

"But we never put it in writing," she twisted the bar towel in her hands, "and now look who's the loser."

Depends on your definition of winning and losing, thought Cassandra. Dead seemed pretty conclusive. "Did you and Jameson talk about the mansion often?"

"Of course, we did! Everyone knows I pour my heart and soul into my businesses. I had plans, you know? Big plans for this town's future," Margie said, passion and hurt in her voice. "And all he cared about was making a profit, tearing down history to make room for generic nonsense. But now... who knows what'll happen."

When exactly had Margie found out about Jameson's change of heart? She always seemed like such a sweet woman, but right now the fire in her eyes was fierce. Could she be capable of cold-blooded murder?

"Margie, we're sorry it turned out this way," Andy said. "We're just trying to piece together a timeline of what happened."

"I already talked to Scott Tate," she replied tersely, clearly unhappy with the situation. "From the questions that youngster asked, you would've guessed he thought I had something to do with it! I've been baking that kid his favorite macaroni and cheese since he was a scrawny little boy."

She took a breath, and Cassandra tried imagining the tall, muscular deputy as a small boy shoveling forkfuls of mac and cheese into his mouth.

"Oh c'mon," the heat in Margie's eyes changed into a mischievous twinkle, "if I did the clown in, I woulda used a poisoned pot pie or something more imaginative than a bullet. But when you find out who killed Jameson, tell them they had every right to be angry."

Cassandra made a mental note not to order the pot pie on her next night out with friends. She was surprised Margie knew that Jameson had died from a gunshot wound when it had happened barely thirty-six hours earlier. Cassandra still wasn't used to the speed of small-town gossip.

"Does this mean you won't be negotiating to buy the property yourself?" It was probably too soon to be asking about that, but she was genuinely curious.

"Pfft," she scoffed. "Unlike Mr. Know-it-All, I am not made of money. I couldn't pull together the pieces to do a deal like that. Why do you think we talked about me leasing space for the bed-and-breakfast? Without Jameson, I haven't got a chance."

Cassandra reached across the table and gently squeezed Margie's arm. "Thank you for your time, Margie." Cassandra signaled to Andy for them to leave. "We should get going."

At least they knew where Margie stood on the topic of Jameson. There wasn't much wiggle room for misunderstanding. She was angry about his untimely passing before their plans were legally cemented. Now, she had no recourse to fulfill her dreams. Margie was passionate about her vision for the town, but would she go as far as murder? It was hard to imagine, but then again, there seemed to be no shortage of people who held grudges against the late Jameson Lee.

As they exited The Home Team bar, Cassandra spotted Derek Swanson leaning casually against a streetlight outside one of the nearby businesses on Main Street. His eyes were glued to Jameson's office across the street, though he tried to appear nonchalant.

"Hey, Derek," Cassandra called out, causing the reporter to lurch around in surprise. "Fancy seeing you here."

"Ah, Cassandra, Andy," Derek replied, standing up a bit straighter. "Just doing a bit of ... freelance work." He was only about five inches taller than Cassandra, yet every time she'd seen him, his pant legs ended well above his ankles, displaying several inches of white athletic socks. Paired with dress shoes, his outfits gave the impression that he had borrowed them from a shorter sibling and had no interest in fashion whatsoever.

"Staking out Jameson's office?" Andy asked, raising an eyebrow.

"Something like that," Derek said, trying to sound as if it was something he did every day. "I figured someone might return to the scene of the crime."

How morbid. The man's body was barely cold. "Except the crime scene was the mansion, not the office," Cassandra pointed out.

"Semantics," Derek waved her statement off. "So, any new leads?"

Cassandra hesitated, knowing she owed Derek for the email he had sent her but not wanting to divulge anything that could get her in trouble with Deputy Tate. He could be a nuisance, but sometimes he had useful information. She glanced at Andy, who nodded almost imperceptibly, giving her the go-ahead.

"Maybe," she said cautiously. "We've talked to a few people, but it sounds like you know as much as we do." She glanced back at the bar and sincerely hoped Margie wasn't involved in anything criminal.

"From what I figure, Patty and Jameson wouldn't win any popularity contests. I think Patty was seeing someone, but no one could tell me the guy's name. Just that she was emotionally touchy in the weeks before she died. Must have been on the down low. Promise if you find anything newsworthy, you'll share," Derek pleaded, clearly hungry for a better story angle.

"You said you're working on a freelance story? Not for the newspaper?"

He shrunk a little, pulling in his shoulders. "The paper laid a few of us off. More of a regional focus now that Lee Energy sold it off to a bigger publisher."

Cassandra didn't even know that Lee Energy also owned a newspaper in Omaha. She thought his businesses were all local. Andy did a low whistle and Cassandra gasped. "I'm sorry about your job, Derek. When did that happen?"

"Last month, for me. It's been in the works a while though. Guess Lee needed all his pennies to buy the mansion. That didn't quite turn out the way he planned, huh?"

His voice held an unmistakably bitter tone. With a curt nod, Andy and Cassandra left him to his amateur detective work and walked down the sidewalk to Andy's Morton Campus Security car.

"I still can't figure out Sean Gill's angle," Cassandra told Andy. "He's obviously not here just to visit his family. But yesterday at the Johnson Mansion, he was all cagey federal super-agent instead of the guy next door."

Andy raised an eyebrow, "Did you want him to be the guy next door?"

She elbowed him in the side while they walked. "Of course not that way. I mean, he looks like Captain America, don't get me wrong. But he wouldn't answer any of my questions about the investigation. And Jameson Lee must have been up to something big if Sean's involved."

Deputy Tate pulled his cruiser to the curb in front of the sheriff's office and met them on the sidewalk. "Please tell me you're not poking around my investigation."

"Jameson Lee was a Morton College donor, and Patty was our student," Cassandra said. "Everything about these crimes relates to the college."

Andy chimed in, "I don't see anyone in handcuffs yet, Scott. We want the same thing as you – to keep the students safe."

"Parents have been calling my office non-stop since Patty's death. We set up a curfew and an escort program so no one has to walk around campus alone."

Tate said, "Those are good moves."

Cassandra crossed her arms. "Was it true that Patty had a boyfriend? I assume you checked for suspicious messages on her phone. Where are you at with suspects and evidence?"

For several moments, Tate stared at her, tight-lipped. He looked like he was considering whether to tell them to back off or ask for their help. "The phone is missing. Wasn't on her body or in her car. She lived alone in a studio apartment. We recovered Jameson Lee's office computer and documents, but it will take time to sort through it all. This is an active investigation. Keep to your lane and let the professionals handle the detective work."

Cassandra nodded, but bit her tongue to keep from asking if the professionals could maybe work a little faster?

Chapter Eight

AS THEY GOT IN Andy's car, Cassandra felt a mixture of frustration and determination. "We've talked to multiple people, but I don't feel any closer to finding Patty and Jameson's killer. My assumption is it's the same person, but that could be mistaken."

Whoever had done this didn't know that Cassandra had the grit of a superhero and wouldn't give up. During their 5K training, she'd discovered one benefit of running was time for ideas to percolate in her head.

"I could use a distraction," Cassandra said. "Let's go back to campus and get Murphy and Buckley. We could meet up for a run. Maybe the break will help us see the situation differently."

"Let's try a different route. I know a neighborhood away from the trails."

An hour later, Cassandra stretched her legs and adjusted her running shoes. "Good call. This is a cute area, and I'm looking for some new landscape ideas. I heard you're supposed to plant some bulbs in the fall so they come up next April?"

Andy smiled. "Four seasons is a big adjustment. Yep, I could come over this weekend and help you plant some tulip bulbs, if you like."

As they began jogging, Cassandra still felt self-conscious about her running abilities. "You know, I haven't been keeping up with the training plan exactly," she confessed, her breath coming out in short huffs. "I feel like a failure for not sticking to it perfectly."

"Don't worry about it," Andy said. "Both our job descriptions require dealing with the unexpected. What matters is that you're still trying and pushing yourself."

Cassandra nodded, feeling slightly better from Andy's positivity. She focused on the rhythmic sound of their footsteps hitting the pavement and the warm sun on her face.

Murphy stopped in his tracks, sniffing at the ground. Before she could stop him, he hunched over and did his business right on a stranger's pristine driveway.

"Murphy, the driveway! Really?" Cassandra exclaimed, mortified. "Oy, what did you eat, bruddah? That pile looks like it came from a Great Dane, not a Westie."

She held out her hand. "I forgot the bags. Can you give me one of yours?"

Andy grimaced, "I forgot the poop bags too. I was too busy making sure I had my music playlist set up that I completely spaced on it."

She scanned frantically for something to clean up with and spotted a discarded pizza box in the home's recycling bin at the curb. She gingerly picked up the pizza box, trying not to touch any of the grease on the bottom. "This is so embarrassing," she muttered as she scooped up the stinking, sloppy mess with the makeshift tool.

When she looked over her shoulder, Andy was doubled over laughing so hard that his palms were resting on his knees. "Leave it to you to MacGyver your way out of this one."

"Next time, I'm carrying a whole box of poop bags in my trunk!"

"Hey, it's all part of the dog mom experience. Learning to adapt to unexpected obstacles is important in both running and life."

Cassandra nodded grimly, gingerly tossing the used pizza box into a different driveway's trash can. "Let's just keep going and see what else this day throws our way."

"One step at a time, right?" Andy moved to fist bump her but pulled his hand back. "Sorry, I'm not touching you after Murphy's surprise explosion just now."

She shook her head. "How do I keep getting myself in these situations ... That's life, I guess. Stinky surprises around every corner."

An hour later, in her small backyard, Cassandra huddled under a tan blanket on the deck writing notes in her bullet journal while Murphy snuffled in the red, orange, and yellow leaves below and marked his presence on the shrubs lining the back fence.

The sunset glowed orange above the trees and reflected off the cloud layers. Crisp, autumn air filled with the scent of pumpkin spice tea swirled around Cassandra's Craftsman-style bungalow. She was so proud of her home, adorned with twinkling orange fairy lights and a smattering of Halloween decorations that peeked out from the front porch in preparation for trick-or-treaters next week.

She squinted at the neighbors' dark and quiet house, wondering how early in the evening retired people went to bed. She spent so many nights on call for work, she wondered if she'd ever learn to stay up past nine or sleep past six, no matter how old she was. Calm moments away from her responsibilities helped keep her balanced. By journaling about the people involved in Patty and Jameson's last days, she hoped to remember important facts or see connections she missed at first.

They'd learned tidbits from many conversations so far, with the exception of Sean Gill. With his superhero jawline and hazel eyes, he was undeniably handsome, but his presence in town always seemed to be shrouded in mystery, which frustrated her to no end.

"Hey, Cassandra!" called a voice from next door. As though she'd conjured him from her imagination, leaning on the corner of her garage, was none other than Sean himself, flashing a smile too charming for the common good.

"Hey, howzit?" she asked, trying to sound nonchalant. She knew better than to pry too much, especially considering their past dustup during the international smuggling case. He had been sent by Homeland Security, and she found herself drawn to the whirlwind of intrigue that always seemed to follow him.

"Your dog was barking up a storm earlier. Thought I'd check in, see if everything's okay."

Cassandra stood on her wooden deck, holding the blanket tight around her shoulders, wearing furry UGG boots and fingerless gloves. Nebraska weather was so weird. It was warm enough just a few hours earlier for her to be out on a run wearing a t-shirt, but now it was cold enough for hibernation.

"Murphy's just... I don't know. He thinks my backyard is his domain and he's the Lion King." She dipped her chin and attempted a James Earl Jones impression: 'Everything the light touches ...'"

They both chuckled at her lackluster dramatic skills. "What about you? Why are you *really* in town?" She had been trying to give him space, but enough was enough.

He sipped from a beer she hadn't noticed he was holding, eyebrows raised in surprise.

"I need some answers," she pressed. "What are you investigating about Jameson Lee and Patty? You can't keep avoiding the subject." Her yard and garage were small enough that they could talk at normal voice levels without bothering the whole neighborhood.

He shrugged, a playful smirk on his face. "Oh, so we're interrogating each other now. I thought you were just here for the falling leaves."

"Very funny, but seriously, I need to know what you're up to. Was Jameson doing some shady business dealings?" Cassandra pressed, not backing down.

"Wow, you really don't let anything go, do you?" he chuckled, shaking his head. "Alright, fine. You want honesty? I'm looking into something, but it's classified. I can't tell you any more than that."

"Classified?" Cassandra scoffed. "You act like you're James Bond or something."

"More like Jason Bourne but without the memory loss," Sean quipped, his eyes twinkling with mischief. "Look, I promise, when I can share more, I will. But for now—"

"Fine," Cassandra interrupted, rolling her eyes. She knew from experience that pushing him further would be fruitless. "But you better keep me in the loop. I don't want any surprises."

"Scout's honor," Sean said, raising his hand in a mock salute. "Now, if you'll excuse me, I have some classified business to attend to."

"Of course," Cassandra replied sarcastically, watching as he disappeared back into his parents' yard. She got it, really. He had a job to do. But so did she. And she'd figure it out with or without Sean Gill's help.

Chapter Nine

C ASSANDRA ENTERED THE CARSON Real Estate office, a converted
Victorian style cottage at the edge of Main Street, her heels
clicking on the polished wooden floor. Her sleek black hair was pulled
into a tight bun, and she wore a crisp, white blouse tucked into her
navy pantsuit. Andy followed closely behind, dressed in his usual
campus security polo shirt and khakis.

Cassandra scanned Loretta Anderson's office interior with clinical
precision. Andy, on the other hand, wore a bemused grin as he glanced
around at the kaleidoscope of colors and patterns that defied logic.
From the mismatched floral wallpaper to the eclectic assortment of
chairs, it was clear that Loretta had a quirky style all her own. In
the corner stood an elaborately decorated umbrella stand, displaying
Loretta's assortment of umbrellas and walking sticks – or were they
wands? The scent of lavender filled the air, emanating from a large
vase of fresh flowers on her desk.

"Ah, Dr. Sato and Mr. Summers!" Loretta exclaimed, jumping up
from behind her desk like a jack-in-the-box. Her voluminous purple
skirt swished around her ankles as she approached them, a large silk
flower clipped atop her head. "I've been expecting you!"

"Hello, Loretta," Cassandra said, offering a polite smile. "Thank you
for seeing us on such short notice."

"Of course, darling!" Loretta replied, waving her hand dismissive-
ly. "Anything for my favorite sleuths! Now, come, have a seat." She
gestured toward the motley collection of chairs, which seemed as
sturdy as doll furniture. With some hesitation, Cassandra and Andy
each chose a sturdy-looking option and sat down.

Scratching the back of her neck, Cassandra marveled at Loretta's complete demeanor change from when they'd bumped into her at the Johnson Mansion, and she'd practically chased them out of the house. This effusive persona was confusing, and frankly spooky.

"Are you sure I can't find you two a place together? You are just the *cutest* couple!"

Embarrassed heat rose up Cassandra's neck to her cheeks, and she didn't dare look at Andy. She'd either bust out laughing at the absurd suggestion or feel a tug at her heart if she saw that puppy-love look he sometimes wore when he thought she didn't notice. Either way, Cassandra kept her eyes fixed straight ahead and answered for them both.

"That's kind of you," she cleared her throat, "but we aren't in the market for a place together."

"That's a shame. But take all the time you need, and I'll be here when you're ready."

"Alright, Loretta," Was it Cassandra's imagination, or did Andy's voice sound higher than usual? He was probably trying not to laugh too. He leaned forward with his elbows on his knees, "We're trying to piece together some information about Lee Energy's connections in the real estate world. We were hoping you might have some insight?"

"Ah, Jameson," Loretta sighed dramatically, placing her hand over her heart. "Such a tragedy, that man. But I can absolutely help you out! Let me just gather my notes." She disappeared behind her desk for a moment, rummaging through piles of papers before triumphantly holding up a folder.

"Here we are!" Loretta announced, striding back to Cassandra and Andy with an air of grandiosity. "Everything you need to know about Jameson's business dealings." As she handed over the folder, Andy's phone buzzed with an incoming text message. He glanced at it and said, "Scott Tate says there's a locked document on Jameson's computer. Just the one. It seems he had something to hide after all. He's asking if someone from the college IT department can help bypass the password." He typed a reply and his phone pinged with the sent message.

"Really? That could definitely change things."

"Indeed," Loretta chimed in, her eyes gleaming with excitement. "Oh, this mystery just keeps getting better and better!"

What was Loretta's angle, besides selling real estate? "How did you end up with the mansion listing?" Cassandra asked. "Was Amanda the only other bidder?"

Loretta chuckled, "Amanda Bauer? Oh hon', she's just my interior decorator. We were measuring for a possible purchaser, but the deal kind of died with Jameson gone. Haven't heard anything from my contact since then."

Andy narrowed his eyes, "So those blueprints at the mansion belonged to Jameson?"

"Oh sugar, I'm like a bulldog when it comes to clients' privacy," she winked. "Don't ask me who drew them. The last time I checked, they were chillin' in my trunk."

"Was your other contact interested in renovation or demolition," Cassandra asked.

The corners of Loretta's mouth twitched, "Mostly renovation talk 'round here—nobody wants to upset the historical or environmental folks. That'd be like poking a hornet nest!" She cackled as if it were an inside joke.

It seemed Margie wasn't alone in not knowing about Jameson's demolition plan. But maybe someone else did.

Just then, Loretta leaned in, her voice hushed to a conspiratorial whisper. "You know, my sister-in-law's niece saw Tom McGinnis snooping around Johnson Mansion late at night. Could he have had a secret rendezvous?" She lifted her can of sparkling water for a subtle sip before continuing. "And don't even get me started on the library director and new school bus driver! They're always sneaking around checking out each other's books... if ya catch my drift."

"I don't need to know," Cassandra held up one hand like a stop sign.

Living in a small town meant people noticed when your car was parked overnight in a driveway that wasn't your own. So far, she'd avoided that predicament herself, and was uncomfortable talking about other people's private lives. "Who knows," Cassandra shifted in her seat. "Tom could have just left his car there after a work meeting. And maybe the librarian's love life isn't our business ..."

As they flipped through the pages in the folder, a particular piece of information caught Cassandra's eye. There, in black and white, was evidence of another property developer who seemed to have had a motive for wanting Jameson out of the picture.

"Wait a minute," she muttered, her pulse quickening. "Andy, look at this."

Cassandra held the folder as if it might contain the answer to all their questions. She couldn't stop her hands from trembling slightly from the excitement.

"Loretta, it looks like another man is mentioned regarding the property. Is this guy, Gerald Wilkins, your client too?"

"He's not a local, as far as I know," Loretta shrugged. "I've only communicated with Mr. Wilkins by emails or phone. When Jameson does deals in Omaha or other towns, I'm not involved. It's such a shame about him. The Johnson Mansion would've been my biggest commission ever," she said wistfully.

"Look at this," Andy said, pointing to a document. "Wilkins purchased a plot of land just days before Jameson was murdered."

A series of transactions indicated that Wilkins had been buying up smaller parcels around the mansion. Without Jameson's cooperation, did he stand to gain easier access to the mansion? That might be a motive for murder. It still didn't explain Patty, but maybe she'd just been in the wrong place at the wrong time.

"Could Wilkins have wanted Jameson out of the way to secure his own development plans?" Cassandra mused, deep in thought.

"Seems likely," Andy agreed. "But why would Jameson work with someone who had such opposing interests?"

"Maybe he didn't know," Loretta chimed in, clearly relishing her role in the investigation. "Or maybe Jameson thought he could outsmart Wilkins."

Andy sighed. "I can't tell if this guy's involvement means anything good for Margie Gallagher. What if Wilkins and Margie were working on a counter offer together and teamed up to get rid of Jameson?"

"Andy!" Cassandra scolded. "How could you think Margie would resort to murder just because she was mad about not getting her bed-and-breakfast?"

Although ... she had to admit that Margie was awfully upset when she found out Jameson planned to raze the place and put in a strip mall.

"I thought we were brainstorming," Andy shrugged. "It's all hypothetical now. Jameson's gone and who knows how long until his estate will be settled."

Cassandra's gaze shifted from the papers in hand to Andy, who had just received a text message. "Alrighty," he said, his grip on the phone tightening, "our IT person managed to open Jameson's secret document. It looks like Jameson was keeping separate notes about his employees, including Patty and Tom."

"His own employees?" Loretta exclaimed, her eyes wide with shock.

"Apparently so," Andy confirmed, scrolling through the information on his phone. "Jameson kept notes on their conversations, meetings, even emails."

"Listen to this," he continued, reading from his phone. "'Tom and Patty romance??' or this one 'Met with Tom today. He seemed more agitated than usual. Asked some strange questions about the mansion, almost like he was probing for weaknesses.'"

"Probing for weaknesses?" Loretta echoed, shivering slightly. "That sounds ominous."

"Maybe Tom saw an opportunity to take over the project himself," Cassandra suggested, her mind racing. "Or maybe he's working with someone else, like this Wilkins guy."

"Either way, we need to find out what Tom's up to," Andy pocketed his phone.

Loretta gathered the documents they'd been looking at. "I'll keep digging into the real estate side of things."

"Thanks, Loretta," Cassandra smiled, grateful for the real estate agent's enthusiasm but still unsure whose team she was really playing on.

"Absolutely, darling," Loretta winked. "I wouldn't miss this for the world."

With their plan in place, Cassandra and Andy stood up to leave the office, determined to uncover Tom's secrets. As they stepped out onto the sidewalk, a sudden gust of wind whipped through the trees, sending leaves swirling around them.

"Feels like something's about to happen," Cassandra murmured, chicken skin running down her arms.

Chapter Ten

THE FOLLOWING MORNING, CASSANDRA decided it was time to compare notes with Sean. She wrapped herself tightly in her plaid scarf and woolen coat, bracing herself against the crisp autumn gusts that sent leaves swirling around her feet.

"Hey neighbor!" she called out as she spotted him sitting on his parents' front porch, sipping coffee from a mug. He looked up and waved, inviting her over with a nod.

"Morning," he greeted her warmly as she approached grasping her coffee mug, Murphy at her heels. "You're up early."

"Every day. I am the definition of a morning person," she quipped, taking the empty chair next to him. "Look, I'm trying to make sense of a few things and want to run them by you. See if anything connects."

Sean nodded in agreement, taking another sip of his coffee. "Sure thing. I'm all ears."

"Alright," she said, organizing her thoughts. "First, we have Jameson Lee, who's known around town for agressive business dealings. Margie Gallagher and others were angry when they found out he reneged on an agreement to renovate the Johnson Mansion. I'm worried that Jameson's intern Patty might have uncovered something that put her in danger. Derek Swanson, the reporter has been investigating Jameson's past. What if Derek is in danger too?"

"Interesting," Sean murmured, his eyes narrowing as he processed the information. "And I assume you've been talking to people around town, getting their take on things?"

"The sheriff's office probably told you that Patty and Tom were mentioned in a secret file on Jameson's computer," Cassandra continued. "Loretta the realtor is a character, but she seems mostly harmless. Did you check out that surveyor I saw the afternoon I found Jameson?"

"He's a real surveyor. Paid by Lee Energy." Sean stroking his chin thoughtfully. "What do we know about Gerald Wilkins?"

"Derek said that Patty may have had a relationship with someone. What if it was this Wilkins? He was a client or partner of Jameson's, so she must have interacted with him."

Sean nodded slowly before replying. "I did a background check on him, but it's a dead end. Before ten months ago, Gerald Wilkins didn't exist."

Cassandra felt a chill, not entirely due to the cold air. The thought of a violent murderer roaming around Carson was unsettling. She tightened her grip around her warm cup of coffee and looked over at Sean.

"Does Andy know about this?"

He shook his head. "Not yet. I'm telling you first. Changing gears, I'm curious about your impression of Lee's assistant, Tom."

"Tom was helpful and friendly," Cassandra said quietly, not sure what Sean wasn't saying directly. "Seemed a bit squirrelly, but smart. I remember one of the notes on Jameson Lee's computer questioned if there was a romance between Tom and Patty. I only saw them in the same room together once before she died, and they didn't act like a couple. But Patty was in full sales mode at the time. If Tom has any connection to Patty's death, we need to know. The sooner, the better."

"Agreed," Sean said, his expression serious. "I'll keep digging on my end and share what I can with you and Andy."

Cassandra was just about to suggest they head back inside when her phone buzzed, with an incoming call-- one from a name she recognized all too well.

"Dr. Sato," Derek Swanson's face beamed from the screen, his eyes alight with excitement. "I think I've got something here."

"Derek," Cassandra hesitated as she glanced around the Gills' front yard, uncertain if she should return inside her house to take the call in private. "What is it?"

"Remember Tom McGinnis that you and Andy were looking into?" He asked, his voice urgent.

"Yes," Cassandra confirmed, her gaze shifting briefly to Sean who seemed equally intrigued.

"Take a look at this." Derek sent through a photo he'd found on Tom's social media. It was an image of a sparkling diamond engagement ring perched atop a red velvet box. "He uploaded it two weeks ago. I did some digging in one of his lesser-known groups to find it." His smug smile revealed his pride at finding such an important clue.

Cassandra studied the image closely, her thoughts racing as she connected dots and formed theories." An engagement ring, huh? Interesting. What makes you think he bought it for someone special?"

"The caption said, 'It's happening.' Do you think it might have something to do with Patty?" Derek suggested, his eyes wide with curiosity.

"Maybe," Cassandra mused, tapping her fingertips against her coffee cup as she thought things through. "But there's no way of confirming anything until we have evidence that they had more than just a work relationship."

"Makes sense," Derek nodded eagerly in agreement, anticipation growing in his expression. "I'll keep looking and see what else I can uncover."

"Nice work, Derek," Cassandra praised, genuinely impressed by his research skills. "Let me know what you find."

"Will do!" He gave her a jaunty thumbs-up before ending the call.

Cassandra stared at the now-dim screen, her thoughts swirling like the leaves in the Gills' front yard. Could the discovery of a potential engagement ring lead them to discover the reason behind the murder? Or was it merely an unrelated coincidence?

"How many of you folks are out here mucking up the sheriff's investigation? Who was that?" Sean asked, his skepticism visible.

"Derek Swanson, a freelance reporter," Cassandra explained. "What he lacks in age or fashion sense he more than compensates for with enthusiasm. He's been doing research for an article about Jameson Lee. He just located a photo of an engagement ring Tom posted on social media."

"An article about Lee? I should probably use Derek as a resource, if he's any good," Sean echoed her earlier sentiment. "But like you said, we can't jump to conclusions without more information."

"Murphy, what do you think?" she asked, turning to her dog who was curled up on the porch beside her chair. The Westie lifted his furry white head and gave her a quizzical look before laying it back down again with a loud sigh that she swore was criticism.

"Thanks for the input, brah," Cassandra muttered sarcastically, rolling her eyes. She sipped her steaming coffee, the rich aroma filling her senses. "For now, I'm focused on gathering intel and seeing where it leads."

"Knowing you, I'm sure it won't take long to figure it all out," Sean said with a smile. "You have a knack for stumbling upon the truth."

"Just admit my stumbling around has purpose and style," Cassandra blushed, not taking his bait. She knew she could trust her instincts, but having Sean's support boosted her confidence.

"Promise me you'll stick to information gathering. Be careful."

Crossing her fingers by her side, she nodded. She was a boring academic, not Wonder Woman. Careful was her middle name.

Chapter Eleven

C ASSANDRA TURNED TOWARD THE back seat of her car, so she could see both Andy and Derek. They'd met after lunch for a final pep talk. "You found lots of good stuff," Cassandra said, pointing to Derek's article on her laptop screen. "Tom attended several conferences on urban development and sustainable living."

"Probably trying to get in good with Jameson's suppliers," Andy mused, sipping his water.

"I think he was planning to use them for his own gain." Derek leaned in closer, squinting at the screen.

"Lee Energy's website says one of the company's current projects is to develop high-end apartments with an arboretum and event space, but it doesn't say where in town it's located." Cassandra said.

"An arboretum, huh?" Andy smirked. "Sounds big city bougie."

"Tom might have more information about Patty's work with Jameson or the other suspects," Cassandra reminded them, her hand hovering over the door latch. "Let's just play it cool and find out what he knows."

Derek nodded in agreement, adding, "The website has been updated since I wrote my article. I'm telling you, there's something off about him. The way he acts like he's smarter than everyone else."

That wasn't the impression Cassandra had gotten from Tom, but then she hadn't talked to him very long before.

Cassandra, Andy, and Derek cautiously entered Lee Energy, their eyes scanning the room for any signs of trouble. They found Tom sitting in the big leather chair that had once belonged to Jameson Lee before his untimely death. Something else about Tom had changed, and it wasn't just his office.

"We need to talk," Cassandra said, her voice firm but cautious.

"By all means, have a seat," Tom replied, gesturing to the chairs opposite his desk. His confident demeanor threw the group off guard. "You three look like you have a lot to say."

As they sat, Cassandra discretely texted Deputy Tate and Sean Gill, asking them to meet her at the office. She also sent Fischer a quick message to let him know what was happening, just in case. Their backup plan was set; now they just needed answers.

"Actually, no," Cassandra replied, keeping her tone even. "We wanted to talk to you about the Johnson Mansion development plan."

"Of course, you would," Tom snorted, rolling his eyes. "I suppose you agree with Councilman Lee and think tearing down that old place was a good idea?" He crossed his arms with an air of self-importance, as if he alone held the key to progress and modernization.

"Actually," Derek interjected, "we're more interested in your plans for it."

Tom's eyes flickered with surprise, but he quickly regained his composure. "My plans? I'm just an assistant, remember?"

Cassandra raised an eyebrow at him sitting in his boss's chair like he owned the place, and Tom had the grace to blush.

"By all means, have a seat," Tom drawled, gesturing to the chairs opposite his desk. His confident demeanor and dismissive attitude threw Cassandra for a loop. "You three look like you have a lot to say."

Cassandra turned away and discretely texted Deputy Tate and Sean Gill, asking them to meet her at the office. She also sent Fischer a quick message to let him know what was happening, just in case. Their backup plan was set; now they just needed answers.

She replied in an even tone as she slid into one of the seats. "Actually no, we wanted to chat about the Johnson Mansion development project."

"Of course, you would," Tom scoffed, rolling his eyes. "I'm sure you agree with Councilman Lee that tearing down the old place was a fantastic idea?" He crossed his arms with an air of self-importance, as if he alone held the key to progress and modernization.

"Actually," Derek cut in, "we're more interested in *your* plans for it."

Tom's eyes flickered with surprise, but he quickly regained his composure. "My plans? I'm just an assistant, remember?"

Cassandra raised an eyebrow skeptically at Tom sitting in his boss's chair like he owned the place. He blushed under her judgmental gaze.

"Cut the act, Tom," Andy warned. "We know you've been attending conferences, cozying up to suppliers, even drawing up blueprints of the mansion."

"Is that a crime?" Tom countered, his voice dripping with sarcasm. "Development doesn't have to destroy the environment. Adding modern amenities while keeping the historical charm is the way of the future."

So, they'd guessed right that the blueprints had belonged to Tom. Did that mean Loretta had been working with Tom instead of Jameson? Cassandra had so many questions.

Cassandra took a deep breath, steeling herself for the confrontation ahead. "Did Mr. Lee know about your plans for the mansion?

"Lee had *plans*, I had a *vision!*" Tom exploded, unable to contain his frustration any longer. "A vision that would benefit everyone! The town council is full of dinosaurs, dragging everyone down. This place needs progress, not sentimentality."

"Since when does progress mean moving into the boss's office just days after his rather convenient death," Andy interjected, standing and leaning over the desk.

His imposing figure loomed over Tom, who visibly swallowed his defiance. For a moment, Cassandra worried that their confrontation might turn physical.

"Ha!" Tom huffed, standing up and pacing around the office. "You have no idea. Jameson Lee would have removed trees, destroyed animal habitat, and put in a lousy strip mall. We take environmental preservation seriously. Under our plan, the mansion would have been transformed into something incredible – high-end apartments with an arboretum, event space, and pickleball courts!"

"Really, Tom?" Cassandra raised an eyebrow. "Pickleball courts?"

"Do you know how hard it is to get a turn on the pickleball courts at the city park?" Tom shouted, gesticulating wildly. "I'm telling you, this would have been huge. Life changing!"

"Life changing for you, maybe," Andy said coldly. "But at what cost to everyone else?"

"Let me ask you something," she chimed in, keeping a safe distance. "If your intentions were so noble, why all the secrecy? Why work behind Jameson's back?"

"Because this town is full of people like you!" Tom shouted. "People who can't see past their own nostalgia. Lee called me a 'young pup' like I was his mascot. But an outsider like Gerald Wilkins starts making waves and suddenly the councilman takes notice."

"And if Gerald Wilkins were to make a deal with Lee Energy, the folks in town would have to respect him," she suggested. "I'm guessing you made up the Gerald Wilkins identity so Councilman Lee would take you seriously. But wasn't there another way to buy the property without resorting to violence?"

"Let's just say I had a different vision for the Johnson Mansion than that ding-dong Jameson," Tom replied cryptically. "I saw opportunity where he only saw cash."

"Is that really all, Tom?" Cassandra asked gently, trying to coax more information from him. "We just want the truth. Tell us more about this vision of yours."

"Fine," Tom sighed, his shoulders dropping as he deflated. "I wanted to create a sustainable community, with green spaces and eco-friendly apartments. A nice place to hold wedding receptions. Believe me, I tried everything."

"Is that why you sabotaged Lee's plans?" Andy asked, his voice low and steady.

"I didn't sabotage anything!" Tom snapped, his defensive posture returning. "No one listened to us. The Mansion should have been my inheritance, but no one in my family took me seriously. When they putting me off after college, I got this job to learn the ropes of the property business. I took my ideas to Mr. Lee, but he wouldn't listen."

He leaned back in the chair, studying them with newfound authority. Gone was the subservient prepster they'd known before; in his place was a man dressed like a Millennial CEO, radiating power and ambition. "Look, I can't say anymore," Tom's mysterious smile widened. "But trust me, it's for the greater good."

Cassandra stared at Tom, her mind racing with everything they knew. The engagement ring on his social media page – could it be his? Who was he seeing? She decided to confront him head-on.

"Tom, we found something interesting on your social media," Cassandra began, showing Tom the engagement ring image. "Is this yours? Are you engaged?"

Tom's face turned a deep shade of red, and his lips curled into a snarl. "That's none of your business!" he barked, slamming his fist on the desk.

Cassandra planted her feet firmly on the ground and squared her shoulders as she faced Tom without flinching; any fear that had been present before was now gone. "Actually, it is our business," she shot back. "We're trying to find out what happened to your coworker and boss, and you seem to know more than you're letting on."

Cassandra heard commotion coming from the main office area and sincerely hoped the cavalry had arrived.

"Tom, calm down," Derek said, attempting to diffuse the situation. "Let's just talk about this rationally."

"Rationally?" Tom sneered. "Patty was the irrational one! So worried about her GPA that she wouldn't take the bold moves I know she wanted! That ring was perfect, just like her. Can't you see I was looking out for our future!"

With no warning, Tom lunged towards Cassandra with his fists balled. She ducked quickly and felt his knuckles brush past her hair as she dodged the attack. Cassandra sidestepped him and grabbed his wrists, using all her strength to hang on.

When Tom yanked an arm free, Andy grabbed it. In the chaos that followed, Cassandra felt a sharp pain in her ribs as she collided with the edge of the desk and crumpled to the floor.

Sean Gill and Deputy Tate rushed into the room and grabbed Tom. "Let's go down the street to our office and talk about this some more. Tom McGinnis, you are under arrest for assault."

"I barely touched her. She tripped!"

"You're also a person of interest in two murders. You have the right to remain silent. ..."

"Hey!" Marcus, who had silently arrived with the police, rushed to Cassandra's side. "Are you okay?"

"Eh ... that would be a no," Cassandra winced as Marcus helped her into the passenger seat of his car, the pain in her ribs making it difficult to breathe. As they drove away from Lee Energy, she clutched her side, silently berating herself for not being more careful.

"Hey," Marcus said gently, reaching over to give her hand a reassuring squeeze. "You're going to be okay. We'll get you checked out while Tom spills his guts to the police."

"Dang," she muttered under her breath, her mind replaying the last twenty minutes. "What a mess."

"When you texted me, I got in touch with Sean. He wasn't thrilled to know y'all were at Lee's main office. Said you'd promised him you'd stay out of it?"

"Not exactly," Cassandra hedged. "I promised to be careful. Andy and Derek were with me."

Marcus's lips formed a thin line. Instead of discussing the reasons for his displeasure at her, she gazed out the window at the passing farms. Her thoughts turned to the Halloween Hustle coming up in less than a week. An ambition that seemed all but impossible with her current injury.

Chapter Twelve

C ASSANDRA WINCED AS SHE shifted the ice pack on her aching ribs, the phone cradled between her ear and shoulder. Her cozy living room, bathed in warm lamplight was a stark contrast to the danger she had recently faced.

"Hey, Andy, the doctor said I have a cracked rib. He gave me some painkillers and a brace to wear for a few weeks," she said, looking down at Murphy who was curled up at her feet, snoring softly. ""I took Murphy out earlier to stretch my legs, and I'm still a bit sore... and my knee hasn't been right since last month. I don't think I can do that 5K race next weekend."

"Come on, Cass," Andy chided playfully. "We trained hard for the run. Just suck it up."

"Easy for you to say," she grumbled. Geesh did she need a doctor's note to get him to back off?

"Anyway," she continued, "let's sum this all up. Tom slash Gerald wanted to turn a haunted mansion into luxury condos with an arboretum and pickleball courts because he had an entitlement complex as a distant relative of the original owners."

"Dude was wackadoodle. Apparently, during the interrogation, Tom confessed something you might find interesting." There was a pause, then Andy continued, "He had a huge crush on Patty. Never told anyone about it, but there was a drawer full of gifts and notes in her office desk. Most of them she didn't even take out of the packaging. In his romantic fantasy, they'd live happily ever after. Super detailed and very one-sided."

"Wow," Cassandra muttered, shaking her head. A sad mix of amusement and revulsion washed over her as she pictured Tom's twisted ambition. "Although, I don't know if 'romantic' is quite the right word for his motives."

"More like delusional," Andy scoffed. "He thought that together, with her smarts and competitive nature, they'd be the next big thing in town. He had a whole scenario planned out where she'd host events and he'd become the real estate hero who saves Carson."

"Yikes," she muttered, trying to imagine the two of them together. The other students had said Patty was ambitious, but this was on another level.

"Tom was disappointed when Patty switched sides and went along with Jameson's plans to demolish the house for a strip mall instead of Tom's luxury condo idea. They found one note from her where she heartlessly rejected his romantic intentions."

"So Tom just decided to kill her?"

"Tom claimed they got into a shoving match, she fell, and hit her head. Of course, without witnesses we'll never know the truth. But Jameson's murder was cold-blooded to seal the real estate deal," Andy confirmed grimly.

Cassandra shook her head at Tom's viciousness. He'd not only allowed Patty to die in pursuit of his real estate dreams, but he had also taken it one step further and killed Jameson Lee to ensure his plans went ahead without a hitch. "Ya know, I just don't understand how people can be so twisted and cruel."

"Hey, at least we got him," Andy reminded her gently. "He won't be hurting anyone else."

"Thankfully," she conceded, trying to focus on the small victories rather than the lingering shadows.

"Exactly," he agreed. "Now ... back to planning our 5K run strategy. All we have to do is cross the finish line. Doesn't matter how slow we go, it's still faster than everyone sitting on the couch. Are you in?"

"I'm in," she agreed, hanging up the phone and stepping outside. The cool evening air washed over her as she led Murphy to the backyard. The sky was a deep shade of indigo, dotted with the first twinkling stars of the night. As Murphy sniffed around for the perfect spot to do his business, Cassandra let her gaze wander across the neighbors' neatly manicured lawn, losing herself in thought.

"Hey Cassandra," came a familiar voice from behind her, causing her heart to jump. She turned to see Sean Gill leaning casually against the corner of her garage separating their yards. "How are you holding up?"

"I'm doing better," she replied, grateful for the company but surprised by his sudden appearance. "Just been... processing everything."

"Understandable," he nodded, his eyes filled with empathy. As they stood there, an unspoken connection seemed to pass between them – a shared understanding of the weight of recent events and the secrets they both carried.

"So, are you done visiting your parents?" Cassandra ventured, though they both knew the question was a euphemism for something else entirely. "With Lee Energy in legal proceedings and Tom in jail, you'll probably head back to DC soon?"

"Sorry I didn't tell you sooner, but you know I couldn't," Sean admitted, the words hanging heavy in the air between them. "We suspected Jameson might be up to something shady. But finding out Tom was responsible for the transactions as Gerald Wilkins ... that part was a surprise."

"We could've worked together, shared information. I can be trusted to use discretion."

"Believe me, I wish I could've confided in you," he said sincerely, his eyes searching hers. "But decisions were made above my pay grade."

"Next time, please keep me in the loop."

Sean looked at her with a wry smile. "I'd like to think there won't be a next time, but trouble seems to find you, Cassandra."

Chapter Thirteen

C ASSANDRA CHECKED HER WATCH, disbelief written across her face. Two miles down, 1.1 to go. Breathing heavily, she looked around at the sea of costumed runners taking part in the Halloween Hustle 5K fun run. A couple dressed as peanut butter and jelly jogged past her, followed by a trio of witches cackling Shakespeare. The course circled around the Morton College campus, and every corner seemed to have a surprise: zombies chasing their next meal, superheroes saving the day, and even a couple of werewolves. She and Andy had opted for plain jogger pants and pullover jackets, not wanting to attract attention to their first awkward run in public.

"Come on," she muttered to herself, "you're like Harry Potter facing the Dementors. Just conjure up an animal Patronus and keep going." Half of her was amazed that she'd made it this far, while the other half was busy trying to ignore the ache of her sore ribs with every deep breath she took. Quitting sounded tempting right now.

Andy jogged alongside her with ease. "Feel free to go ahead," she told him between breaths, not wanting to slow him down. Secretly, she knew it would be easier to stop and walk or even quit if he weren't there watching.

"Are you kidding?" Andy grinned as he teased her, "If I leave you, who's going to make sure you don't collapse? Besides, don't you remember our steak dinner bet? You're giving up on the free beer that easily?"

"Don't make me laugh," she clutched her side. "No really. Don't make me laugh. It hurts too much."

"Consider me your personal comedian," Andy quipped, keeping a steady stream of puns and campus anecdotes flowing. Despite the pain, Cassandra found herself cracking smiles and attempting not to outright giggle. His ceaseless banter provided enough distraction for her to muster up some motivation and keep pushing through to her goal.

The last quarter mile of the race stretched before Cassandra and Andy like a gauntlet, with Main Street lined by cheering spectators. Colorful posters waved in the air, emblazoned with encouraging messages like "You're almost there!" and "Run like you're being chased by zombies!" The energy was infectious, and even through her exhaustion, Cassandra felt her spirits lift.

As they turned the final corner, the massive blow-up finish line loomed in the distance, a giant black cat arching its back, the timer ticking away beneath it.

"Almost there," Andy huffed, his breath creating little puffs of steam in the crisp, autumn air.

Cassandra gritted her teeth, focusing on putting one foot in front of the other. As they passed an elderly couple holding a sign that read, "You're running better than our government!" Cassandra smiled through her pain.

Together, they made it through the final stretch, crossing the finish line in unison. Andy bumped her fist, "We did it!"

"Never doubted it for a second," she lied, gasping for breath. Despite her exhaustion, a surge of pride washed over her.

"Way to go," Marcus Fischer called out, jogging over to greet them. His smile was warm and genuine as he wrapped his arms around Cassandra. "You really did it."

"Thanks," she replied, leaning into his embrace, grateful for his support.

Out of the corner of her eye, she noticed Sean Gill watching from a distance, an enigmatic expression on his face. There was a hint of envy in his gaze, but also something akin to respect and acknowledging her current relationship with Marcus. She didn't have time to think about what his look meant, but she'd save it away for a quiet time when she could mull it over more.

Later, with the sun sinking lower in the sky, Cassandra and Andy celebrated their success at The Home Team bar. The late afternoon sun cast everything in a warm and inviting golden hue, while they chose a table outside on the patio so that Murphy and Buckley could join them for dinner.

Nearby a group of students chatted loudly, their table covered with pints of beer, and mounds of appetizers. Two of them waved at her and she recognized them from her office.

"Congrats on surviving the 5K, Dr. Sato," Bridget said, "Logan had to admit defeat and pay the penalty."

"You bet against me?"

"Well, you were hurt, and we thought you'd bail on the run. But then we saw you whizzing by Johnson Mansion," Logan said, "did you spot any ghosts?"

"Nah, I'm way too fast for those ghosts to catch me!" Cassandra joked.

"Great job out there, you two!" Margie Gallagher beamed as she approached their table, balancing a plate of onion rings on one hand. "These are on the house as appreciation for catching Tom."

"Thank you, Margie," Cassandra replied, accepting the basket of golden-fried treats. She knew her healthier eating habits would have to start tomorrow but couldn't resist indulging on such a special occasion.

"Maybe I should keep running," Andy joked, popping an onion ring into his mouth. "That way, I can still eat my favorites without guilt."

"Speaking of plans," Margie said, her eyes sparkling, "the town council will be discussing a new partnership for the town to purchase the Johnson Mansion and lease it to community businesses. I may get my bed-and-breakfast yet. Fingers crossed!"

"Best of luck, Margie," Cassandra said sincerely. "You deserve it."

As they sipped their drinks and laughed together, Cassandra looked around at the buildings around the patio. The sun was setting, casting long shadows across the courtyard, and she felt a sense of contentment settle over her. After tragedy now it was time for healing and growth both for Carson and for herself.

Murphy nudged Cassandra's leg, his eyes pleading for affection. She reached down and gave him a gentle scratch behind the ears, her heart swelling with love for the once-difficult dog. She couldn't imagine her life without him.

"Hey brah," she murmured, "we make a pretty good team, don't we?"

"Ya know, I used to think wellness was just about bubble baths and candles," she confessed to Andy. "But now I see it's so much more. It's also about balance, mindfulness, and knowing when to take a step back."

"Cheers to that," Andy raised his glass, clinking it against hers. "Here's to new beginnings, for all of us,"

"New beginnings," Cassandra agreed. And as the sun dipped below the horizon, she felt an overwhelming sense of gratitude for the twisting, turning journey that had led her here.

"Here's to us, Murphy," she whispered, scratching behind his ears as he wagged his tail. "And to all the adventures yet to come."

About the Author

photo credit: Susan
Noel

Kelly Brakenhoff is an American Sign Language Interpreter whose motivation for learning ASL began in high school when she wanted to converse with her Deaf friends. She divides her writing time between the Cassandra Sato Mystery Series and a children's picture book series featuring Duke the Deaf Dog. She serves on the Board of Editors for the Registry of Interpreters for the Deaf publication, *VIEWs*, and the Steering Committee for the Guppy chapter of Sisters in Crime. A wife, mother of four young adults and a hunting dog, and proud grandma, Kelly and her husband call Nebraska home. Subscribe to her monthly newsletter from her website: kellybrakenhoff.com

What's next?

It's time to gear up for *Homecoming*, the upcoming fifth book in the series! Cassandra Sato is back and headed to her island home. She'll be leading a group of students on Morton College's summer study trip to Hawaii. But it won't be all sunshine and sandy beaches—there's an ancient legend to explore, secrets to uncover, and clues left behind by her ancestors that will make this summer unlike any other. Will she stay in her island home, or will her new life in Nebraska call her back? Pack your bags with Cassandra this summer as she embarks on the journey of a lifetime – *Homecoming*. Coming 2024!

Also By Kelly Brakenhoff

CASSANDRA SATO MYSTERIES
Dead End (Short Story)
Death by Dissertation
Dead Week
Dead of Winter Break
Scavenger Haunt (Short Story)
Death 101: Extra Credit
Halloween Hustle (Novella)
Homecoming (coming in 2024)

DUKE THE DEAF DOG ASL SERIES
Never Mind
Farts Make Noise
My Dawg Koa
Sometimes I Like the Quiet
Duke the Deaf Dog Workbooks Ages 3-5
Duke the Deaf Dog Workbooks Ages 6-9